PATRICIA THAYER
The Cowboy's Adopted Daughter

THE BRIDES
of
BELLA ROSA

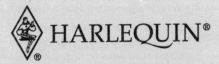

HARLEQUIN®

TORONTO • NEW YORK • LONDON
AMSTERDAM • PARIS • SYDNEY • HAMBURG
STOCKHOLM • ATHENS • TOKYO • MILAN • MADRID
PRAGUE • WARSAW • BUDAPEST • AUCKLAND

Recycling programs
for this product may
not exist in your area.

ISBN-13: 978-0-373-17674-8

THE COWBOY'S ADOPTED DAUGHTER

First North American Publication 2010.

Copyright © 2010 by Harlequin Books S.A.

Special thanks and acknowledgment are given to Patricia Thayer for her contribution to THE BRIDES OF BELLA ROSA series.

Printed in U.S.A.

"You're scared. You trusted your husband and he let you and Cherry down." His gaze held hers. *"I'm not him. I want to try to prove it to you. We need a chance to see where this leads. I won't let you down. Don't desert me now."*

"Oh, Alex." She had trouble keeping a clear head.

His mouth closed over hers, tasting the traces of her mint toothpaste. He drew her closer, holding her against him as if she would disappear. He couldn't let that happen—not now and, if he had the opportunity, not ever.

When he finally pulled back, he saw the want and need in her pretty emerald eyes. "A couple of days, Allie," he said. "Give me a couple of days—that's all I ask. I promise you and Cherry will enjoy it."

She rewarded him with a smile. "My daughter is a pushover." She wrapped her arms around his neck. "It's me you have to convince, cowboy."

He smiled, too. "I'll do my best, ma'am." His head lowered to hers and he did as he promised.

THE BRIDES of BELLA ROSA

Romance, rivalry and a family reunited.

For years Lisa Firenzi and Luca Casali's
sibling rivalry has disturbed the quiet, sleepy Italian
town of Monta Correnti, and their two feuding
restaurants have divided the market square.

Now, as the keys to the restaurants are
handed down to Lisa's and Luca's children,
will history repeat itself? Can the next generation
undo its parents' mistakes, reunite the families
and ultimately join the two restaurants?

Or are there more secrets to be revealed?

*The doors to the restaurants are open,
so take your seats and look out for secrets,
scandals and surprises on the menu!*

The Brides of Bella Rosa saga
continues next month in

Passionate Chef, Ice Queen Boss
by Jennie Adams

Originally born and raised in Muncie, Indiana, **Patricia Thayer** is the second of eight children. She attended Ball State University, and soon afterwards headed West. Over the years she's made frequent visits back to the Midwest, trying to keep up with her growing family.

Patricia has called Orange County, California, home for many years. She not only enjoys the warm climate, but also the company and support of other published authors in the local writers' organization. For the past eighteen years she has had the unwavering support and encouragement of her critique group. It's a sisterhood like no other.

When not working on a story, you might find her traveling the United States and Europe, taking in the scenery and doing story research while thoroughly enjoying herself accompanied by Steve, her husband for over thirty-five years. Together they have three grown sons and four grandsons. As she calls them, her own true-life heroes. On rare days off from writing, you might catch her at Disneyland, spoiling those grandkids rotten! She also volunteers for the Grandparent Autism Network.

Patricia has written for over twenty years and has authored more than thirty-six books for Silhouette and Harlequin Books. She has been nominated for both the National Readers' Choice Award and the prestigious RITA® Award. Her book *Nothing Short of a Miracle* won an *RT Book Reviews* Reviewer's Choice award.

A long-time member of Romance Writers of America, she has served as president and held many other board positions for her local chapter in Orange County. She's a firm believer in giving back.

Check her Web site at www.patriciathayer.com for upcoming books.

To the Scissor Sisters,

Michele Braithwaite, Lindsay Fulmer,
Amy Lawrence, Barbara Marshburn,
Karren Mitchell, Margaret Russell, my sister-in-law,
Pat Wright and Kay Yu Kim for letting me visit
your group, and answering all my questions.

You sure aren't your grandmother's quilting bee.

CHAPTER ONE

ALEX CASALI sat atop his stallion, Diablo, as he looked at the pasture below where three hundred head of prime Herefords grazed contently. In another few months the herd would be moved again at fall roundup, and the yearlings shipped to his feedlot outside Kerry Springs.

He shifted in the saddle and looked over the hill country. With each season came the familiar routine he needed to keep order in his life. He glanced around the hundreds of acres that made up his ranch. In Texas, his cattle operation was considered average, except the A Bar A Ranch purebred steers weren't average. Casali beef demanded top dollar, and got it.

It had taken years of hard work and struggle to get a piece of Texas land. He'd hired on to several cattle outfits and saved every dime for his own place. Little by little he'd restored this once rundown ranch he'd bought at auction until it suited his tastes. After ten years and some good investments, he'd built an empire.

He leaned his forearm against the saddle horn. Yet, the Casali Cattle Company wasn't enough to satisfy him. He'd begun breeding horses a few years back. Now, another new venture. He'd soon be opening a guest ranch. He looked past the grove of trees at the dozen new cabins that would soon be open to strangers.

He had to be crazy for letting Tilda talk him into this project. Yet, his one-time housekeeper, ranch book-keeper—and now partner in the guest ranch—had come up with some good ideas over the years to stimulate revenue. It still didn't change the fact that what he liked the most about this life was the solitude, having no need to be around many people. Outside of his brother, Angelo, he preferred to be alone.

Diablo danced impatiently and Alex tugged on the reins to get him under control. That was when he caught sight of a vehicle coming down the main road toward his house.

He didn't recognize the car. That meant they had no business on his land.

Allison Cole glanced out of the window as she drove her small SUV through the large stone and wrought-iron archway announcing the A Bar A Ranch. Cedar and oak trees lined the narrow road from the hot sun. Rows of pristine white rail fences ran alongside the road as horses roamed contentedly in the grassy pastures.

"This is really something, isn't it, Cherry?"

She glanced into the rear-view mirror to see her daughter watching the countryside from her safety seat. Most four-year-olds were inquisitive and asked a lot of questions. Not Cherry. And Allison missed hearing her child's tiny voice. Outside of her cries in the night, Cherry hadn't talked since the accident. Nor had she walked.

When Tilda Emerson called her early this morning, Allison couldn't turn down her intriguing invitation. Coming here today was for her daughter, as much as for the new business she was trying to launch in town, her quilt shop, Blind Stitch. So she dropped everything, packed up Cherry and drove out here to meet Tilda.

It had been a long time since she'd taken a leisurely afternoon off. On impulse, Allison pulled the car to the side of the road where several horses and foals were grazing in the high grass.

"Cherry, you want to see a horse?"

Ignoring the silence, Allison got out and removed her daughter from her seat. Lifting the small child in her arms, she carried her to the fence.

She was encouraged as her daughter gripped the rail and looked over at the animals. There was awareness in the child's eyes that hadn't been there for a long time.

"See the baby horse?"

"What do you think you're doing?"

At the sound of a deep voice, Allison swung around. A large man was sitting atop a very large horse. The bright sunlight was behind him, making it impossible to see anything except the outline of his wide shoulders and cowboy hat.

It was hard not to be intimidated. "I'm sorry. What did you say?"

The black stallion danced sideways and blew out a breath. "You're on private property," he said. "That's called trespassing."

"No. I was invited to come here. I have a business meeting with Tilda Emerson."

Although she couldn't see his eyes, she felt his gaze locked on her.

"She's up at the house. I suggest you don't keep her waiting." With that he wheeled the horse around and took off.

"Not a friendly man," she murmured. After strapping

Cherry back into her safety seat she headed back to the narrow road. Maybe coming here wasn't such a good idea.

Allison drove past several outbuildings, including a huge red barn and attached corral. Then she saw the large, two-story, brick and clapboard home. Black shutters stood out from the glossy white siding, and the wraparound porch was highlighted by hanging baskets of flowers.

"Really something," she murmured again, recalling the luxury home she'd left back in Phoenix. Per instructions from Mrs. Emerson, Allison passed up the circular drive in front of the house and parked by the back door.

Shutting off the engine, she turned to Cherry. "We're not going to stay long, sweetheart." She reached back and brushed the strawberry-blonde curls away from her daughter's face. Those big blue eyes looked back at her, but her child didn't respond, just turned her head and stared out of the window.

Allison looked past a large oak tree and saw a horse grazing just beyond the fence.

"Look, Cherry, another horse."

Allison climbed out of the car just as a woman stepped out of the house. About sixty, she was tall and slender, dressed in a pair of jeans and a colorful blouse.

"Mrs. Emerson?"

The gray-haired woman smiled as she came down the porch steps. "It's Tilda. You must be Allison Cole. So glad you could make it."

They shook hands. "Well, you made me curious with your proposal. I'd like to hear more."

"Good. Did you have any trouble finding the place?"

Allison thought back to the cowboy. "I ran into one of the ranch hands and he gave me directions." She glanced back into the car. "I hope you don't mind that my daughter came along."

Tilda waved a hand. "There's no reason why you shouldn't bring her. Let's get her out of the hot car."

Allison hesitated, then she popped the SUV's hatch, revealing the small wheelchair. "Let me get Cherry settled, and then we can talk."

The older woman's smile wavered. "Here, let me help you."

Together they got out the chair and Allison lifted her daughter into the seat.

Tilda led them to a shaded patio area just down from the porch. "Cherry, that's a pretty name and you're a pretty little girl," she said. "Do you like animals?" Even without a response, the older woman continued on, "I hope so. We've got plenty of them around here."

As if her words were magic, a large dog wandered over, followed by another smaller one.

"This big guy is Rover." She stroked the black Labrador mix. "The little one is Pete." She also gave some attention to the Heinz 57 variety of a mutt. "They like to be petted by little girls and boys." On cue Rover wandered over and laid his head on the arm of the wheelchair.

Allison was shocked when her daughter placed her small hand on the animal. Pete soon wanted attention and rose up on his hind legs and danced around. Cherry petted him, too.

After getting her daughter some lemonade, Allison went inside to the big open kitchen.

"I should bring Cherry inside, too."

Tilda brought two glasses to the table. "I doubt she wants to leave her new friends. Relax, we can see her from the window. Rover and Pete will keep an eye on her."

With a nod, Allison sat at the table next to the picture window. With her daughter in full view, she turned to Tilda. "You have a beautiful place."

"Why, thank you, but it's not mine. Not any more, that is. When my husband died twelve years ago, I couldn't manage the ranch on my own, and I couldn't afford to hire anyone. It got pretty run-down. Finally the bank took it and sold it at auction to Alex Casali."

"I'm sorry, that had to be awful."

"It was for the best. Besides, Alex asked me to stay on. I took care of the house, helped with the bookkeeping. He's accomplished a lot in the past ten years. He's restored this house, built a new barn and outer buildings for his prime cattle operation. This ranch is a showplace again. I'd like to think I helped with that." She grinned. "Now, I'm a partner in this new project of the guest ranch."

"I have to be honest, Tilda. I might not be able to put the time needed into this project." Allison knew she was crazy to nix this chance. She could use the income. "I can't take the time away from my daughter."

The older woman nodded. "I expect we can work something out because I believe you're perfect for what I have in mind."

At the barn, Alex handed Diablo's reins off to Jake, one of the ranch hands, then headed toward the house. That was when he saw the woman's car at the back door. Great. Tilda's visitor was probably the decorator for the cabins. Who needed to decorate log cabins? He didn't want any part of picking wall colors or curtains. He'd just go inside, give a nod of greeting to the striking redheaded woman with the haunting green eyes, then go off to the office.

Easy.

He'd been attracted to women before but walked away, especially when they had commitment written all over them. This one had a child.

He started up the porch steps when he spotted an empty wheelchair next to the slatted fence. When he got closer, he saw the dogs, along with Buckshot, just on the other side of the fence. Nothing strange about that, but they had company. The little girl he saw earlier.

"What the hell?" He went over and slipped through the railings to find the child sitting on the ground next to the fence. Old Buckshot's head was down so she could pet his muzzle. This was not a good idea.

"Well, damn," he said under his breath. The little sprite heard and turned to him. Her sky-blue eyes were wide with excitement as she smiled at him, her head a crown of strawberry-colored ringlets.

"Horsey," she whispered.

His chest tightened. "Yeah, he sure is." Not wanting to frighten the kid, he made slow, easy movements. "How 'bout I lift you up so you can pet the old gray better."

He was taken by surprise when the girl raised her arms toward him. A strange feeling went through him as he picked up the small child as if she didn't weigh anything. With her secure in his arms, he took her to the animal's side so she could touch him.

"His name is Buckshot. He likes to be petted here." He took her tiny hand and placed it on the horse's head.

Alex was rewarded with a tiny giggle. Another sensation stirred in his chest.

Suddenly he heard a woman's cry. "Cherry!"

Alex turned in time to see the kid's mother running

from the house. Her long auburn hair was flying around her face as she hurried toward the fence. She ducked through the slats. Suddenly her shapely bottom became his focal point with her efforts to get into the pasture. She finally got untangled and stood in front of him. The top of her head only reached the middle of his chest.

"Cherry." She took her child from him. "Are you all right?"

He didn't like the look she gave him. "Thanks to me she is."

The woman turned her attention to him, pinning him with a jade-green stare. "I don't appreciate you taking my child in here without my permission."

"Lady, I didn't take her anywhere," he said, pointing toward the ground. "I found her right in this spot with Buckshot."

The mother glared back. "That's impossible. Cherry can't walk."

Alex glanced at the child, wondering what had happened. "Well, however she got here, I didn't bring her."

"Then how?"

Alex shrugged. "Ask her."

Suddenly tears filled her eyes. "I would love to, but my daughter hasn't spoken in a year."

"She spoke to me," he told her. But as if to call him a liar, the girl refused to say anything.

They both stared at the child. "Cherry? Do you like the horsey?" her mother asked. The child looked back to the horse, but didn't say a word.

Finally Tilda appeared, causing Alex to wonder where she'd been all this time. "Sorry, I had to take that call. Is everything okay?"

Allison continued to glare. "Seems I'm having a

disagreement with your ranch hand. Something he knows nothing about."

Alex refused to be baited by this woman. "Maybe you don't know your child as well as you think."

"How dare you?"

Tilda stepped in. "Stop! This was my fault. I'm the one who said she'd be fine on the patio." She looked concerned. "I'm sorry, Allison, I had no idea she would wander off."

Alex looked at the woman, unable to ignore her appeal. "And I'd appreciate it if you stayed with your daughter from now on. A ranch isn't the best place to leave kids unsupervised."

Allison turned to Tilda. "How do you put up with this?"

"It's hard sometimes," Tilda said as her mouth quirked as if hiding a smile. She shot him a glare. "Allison Cole, this is Alex Casali, the owner of the A Bar A."

Allison hated that the man was so smug. She also hated that she noticed he was so handsome. That was, if you liked the tall, muscular, rough type of guy with piercing gray eyes.

"At a loss for words, Mrs. Cole?"

She'd forgotten arrogant. "My concern is for my daughter, Mr. Casali." She shifted Cherry higher on her hip. "She's usually shy around strangers."

He pushed back his black cowboy hat, revealing light brown hair. "That's understandable." He glanced at Cherry and his expression softened. "She's sure not afraid of animals."

Cherry made a grunting sound and pointed toward Buckshot, then reached out toward Alex Casali.

Allison tried to hold her back, but the uneven weight

threw her off balance. Alex had no choice but to take the determined child.

He easily lifted her daughter into his arms. "Do you mind?" he asked.

She shook her head. This had been the most response she'd seen from Cherry since before the accident. "Please be careful with her."

He gave her a stony look. "I'd never be anything else."

Alison watched closely as he carried Cherry over toward the horse.

Tilda came up to her. "You don't have to worry about old Buckshot," she said. "He was my husband's horse, and a darn good cutter, too. As they say, he's been put out to pasture to live out his days. And besides, Cherry's got some pretty strong arms holding her."

"Horses are so big."

"You're right. Even though Buckshot is gentle, he's still a large animal. But Alex will make sure she's safe." Tilda nodded toward the two dogs following after her. "Your daughter has made many friends today."

Allison wasn't looking at the horse or the dogs, but at the man holding Cherry. As big as he was, he was gentle with her. And most importantly, her daughter seemed to trust him. Not that either of them had much reason to trust when it came to men.

"I know Alex is a little rough around the edges," Tilda began, "but he's got a good heart." The older woman smiled. "What's most important is Cherry thinks so."

Before Allison could say anything, the rancher turned and started back toward them. Her daughter's head rested contentedly on his broad shoulder, her eyes closed. "I think someone's tired."

"Well it's no wonder with the time she's had," Tilda said. "Let's take her inside and put her down."

Allison hesitated. "Maybe we should head back to town."

Tilda shook her head. "Why put her in a hot car? We have a comfortable bed close by. Then we can finish our talk."

Without getting permission, Alex Casali started for the paddock gate. Allison ran after him. "I didn't agree to stay."

"I don't know where you come from, but here in Texas we don't turn down hospitality when it's offered." He kept his hand on the child's back and his strides were steady and smooth. "Me, I can care less if you stay, but your visit is important to Tilda."

"It's important to me, too."

He stopped at the steps to the porch. "Then it's settled, you stay and talk with Tilda."

She fisted her hands, but kept her voice low and controlled. "My concern, Mr. Casali, is my daughter. She's been through a rough year."

"It's Alex. And I can see that, but I can also see this little one was enjoying herself a few minutes ago."

Okay, he had her there. "All right, we'll stay."

With a nod, he went up the steps and she followed behind. Tilda arrived and rushed on ahead, through the kitchen and pantry, then into a good-size bedroom containing a double bed. She pulled back the bright patchwork quilt.

Allison's heart ached, watching the large man gently place her tiny daughter on the mattress, her lifeless legs at a funny angle. When Alex stepped away, she quickly shifted Cherry's body onto her side, and draped a thin blanket over her. After brushing away a few soft curls from her baby's flushed face, she turned to find the rancher had already left. She followed Tilda out and back into the kitchen. Her daughter's rescuer wasn't there, either. To her surprise she was disappointed by his disappearance.

CHAPTER TWO

ALLISON walked across the kitchen to the table. She knew Tilda wanted to discuss business, but her mind kept wandering elsewhere. Where had Alex Casali gone? And would he be back to sit in on the discussion? More importantly, did he want her here?

Tilda brought two fresh glasses of lemonade. "We'll be able to hear Cherry if she wakes up. So sit and relax."

"Thank you." Allison took a long drink.

The older woman took the seat across from her. "I guess I'm not making much of a first impression."

"No, it's not your fault, Tilda," Allison said. "I probably should have explained the situation and asked you to meet at the shop. It's easier for Cherry."

The woman studied her a moment. "If you don't mind my asking, has your daughter always been in a wheelchair?"

She shook her head. "No. She was in an automobile accident last year and she hasn't been able to walk since."

Tilda's aged hand covered hers. "That has to be so hard on both of you."

Allison swallowed hard, feeling a growing connection with this woman. Since her grandmother's passing,

Allison really hadn't had anyone to talk to. "It was touch and go for a while. Although the surgeon repaired the damage to Cherry's spine, she needs a lot of therapy. Even then, there aren't any guarantees for a full recovery."

Tilda smiled sadly. "Well, as long as there's hope. She seemed happy around the animals."

Allison shook her head, amazed. "I'm confused. I'm usually the only one she wants."

"Alex might be a man of few words, but he's the best with animals…and it looks like kids, too."

Definitely not adults, Allison thought.

"Feel free to tell me to mind my own business," Tilda began, "but what about Cherry's father?"

"He's not in our lives anymore." And that was all she was going to say about it.

"It's a tough job, being a single parent."

"All I want is for Cherry to be a typical, happy kid again." Tears threatened. "She hasn't spoken since the accident."

Tilda sighed. "Oh, bless her."

Allison thought back to the corral, seeing her daughter reach out for Alex Casali. A perfect stranger and a man, no less.

"Today, Rover, Pete and Buckshot seemed to get a big response from her," Tilda said. "You're welcome to bring Cherry back any time. If you decide to do the quilting retreat, she can spend time with them every day."

"Oh, Tilda, I don't see how I can oversee a workshop and care for my daughter, too. And there's my shop in town."

"Cherry's welcome. She can join us and you'll have plenty of time to spend with her. And as for your shop, can't Mattie handle running it for a few days?"

Allison had been lucky to find Mattie Smyth, a widow who had time on her hands. But Tilda's offer was tempting, too. "Five days is a long time."

Tilda leaned forward. "We can make adjustments on the time if needed." She sighed. "Look, Allison, the straight talk is, the Hidden Hills Guest Ranch is a new venture for us. Let's just say Alex wasn't keen on my idea of bringing people here. He's more into his cattle and horses. Besides the money to be made in this venture, I'm going to enjoy having people around. And truth is, Alex needs it, too."

Allison would second that. The man didn't seem to have many social skills.

"So if I can make this retreat work," Tilda continued, "my plan is to eventually have several different events going on during the year."

Allison was impressed with this woman's business savvy, and also tempted.

Tilda continued, "Kerry Springs has become a popular retirement community. There are a lot of seniors who aren't ready to just sit around, including several women from my church who want to attend the quilting classes."

Allison certainly missed designing her quilt patterns and doing her weekly cable program. Yet, a demanding career had cost her the early years with Cherry. A lesson she had learned nearly too late. Never again would she get back into that rat race of long days and travel. "What level of classes are you talking about?"

Tilda shrugged. "I've advertised it for experienced quilters, but we aren't turning anyone away. Many of the women were fans of your television program, *Quilt Allie*. They've even used some of your quilt patterns."

Allison glanced away, recalling the reason she'd had

to walk away from her lucrative career. "I gave up the show after Cherry's accident. She needs me to be a full-time mom." And her ex-husband got the income from sales of all her previous quilt designs. She'd given Jack Hudson everything to get the divorce and permanent custody of her daughter. Since Cherry's care was costly, she could use some extra income.

Allison looked at Tilda. "I'll need to have two after-noons off so I can take Cherry to therapy."

"Not a problem. And you'll have your own cabin during the retreat. You won't even have to drive back to town, unless you want." When Tilda named the salary, Allison knew she had to try and make it work.

The brooding Alex Casali flashed in her head. The man didn't even seem to like her, but she doubted he'd get involved in a quilting workshop.

Allison released a breath. "Then as long as Cherry can come with me, we should be able to work something out. But first, I need to talk to Mattie about working longer hours."

"Of course." Tilda's eyes brightened and she stood. "I know Mattie will do this. Would you mind if I called her?" She left the room before Allison could stop her.

Allison got up and looked around the big country-style kitchen. It had been remodeled with maple cabinets and granite counters, but it still had a warm, cozy feeling. The aroma of spices coming from the oven made her think of her grandmother. Their home hadn't been close to this grand. It had just been a small two-bedroom rental with noisy pipes and squeaky floors. But Emmeline Cole had given her love and a roof over her head when no one else wanted her.

Later on, Allison had been just as eager for love when

she'd picked a husband. Jack had other ideas on what marriage meant.

Allison went to a window and looked out at a picturesque scene of the large ranch operation. She hoped Cherry understood her reason for doing this, remembering sitting at her bedside fifteen months ago. All the time she'd begged her daughter to wake up, she'd promised she'd be a real mother to her from now on.

Cherry had held her accountable to her words and had been possessive since the accident. Until today when she practically jumped into Alex Casali's arms.

Allison heard steps and turned around. It wasn't Tilda returning, but Alex who walked into the kitchen.

Speak of the devil. Her breath caught as her gaze moved over the man. He'd showered and shaved and, now he was minus the black hat, she got a good look at the startlingly handsome cowboy. He was getting an eyeful, too. She felt a strange tingling of awareness through her body.

"Surprised you're still here," he said, then went to the coffee pot and poured a cup.

"We'll be leaving as soon as Cherry wakes up."

He took a drink from the mug as he leaned back against the counter, his booted feet crossed at the ankles. "Makes no difference to me. It's just that Tilda wants the guest ranch to go off without a hitch. So if it's more money you want—"

So far everything out of this man's mouth had irritated her. "Her offer is more than fair. I only have to make sure I can care for my daughter."

He nodded. "Good. The little one will probably enjoy coming out here." He pulled her back to his steel-gray gaze. "That is, unless you're afraid to let her be around animals."

"Until today, Cherry hasn't been near a horse. I had no idea that she'd respond so strongly."

He put down his mug and pushed away from the counter. "Then you shouldn't deny her the pleasure of visiting Buckshot. Some say horse therapy helps kids. Maybe she'll even be able to ride someday."

She tensed. "Wait a minute. I didn't say anything about letting her ride. She can't even walk…yet."

"She may not be able to walk, but she's figured out how to get what she wants."

He crossed the room to her and she felt her breath catch in anticipation. "What about you, Allie? You brave enough to go after what you want?"

Alex couldn't figure out why this woman got to him. He should just walk away and leave this all to Tilda. Instead he kept coming back to the pretty redhead.

"Brave or not, Mr. Casali, my only concern is to be a good mother to my daughter. I'm teaching this workshop for that reason and that reason only. So don't let me keep you from what you have to do." She turned to the window. "Don't you have some cattle to brand, or round up somewhere?"

Although she tried to hide it, he could see that she was uncomfortable with him.

"Not at the moment."

"Well, don't let me stop you from your work."

"You aren't." He put his mug in the sink. "I've been up since four a.m. so my chores are finished."

"I thought ranchers worked from sunup to sundown."

"Not if we can help it. And there are ranch hands that help out, too."

Before Allison could answer him, Tilda came into the

room with the phone against her ear. She was smiling. "She's right here." Tilda held out the receiver to Allison. "It's Mattie."

She took it, then walked away. Alex turned to Tilda. "Any problems?"

"None at all. Looks like we got Allison Cole," she said.

Alex studied the petite woman in the dress trousers and leather pumps and prim white blouse. City. "You sure she's going to fit in here?"

Tilda looked at him. "Of course. Why wouldn't she? Besides, Allison is from the country, Virginia, I think." She placed her hands on her hips. "Why are you suddenly interested? I thought you didn't want any part of this project."

"I don't but I more or less got thrown into it when I rescued the kid from the pasture."

A spark lit in her hazel eyes. "Cherry is cute, isn't she? The mother's not so bad, either."

He didn't want to have this discussion, but that didn't stop Tilda.

"I don't think I've seen hair that rich auburn color before," she went on, "And those freckles across her face are cute. I think her best feature are those green eyes."

The last thing he needed to do was think about Allison Cole. "I've got paperwork." He started to leave, but she stopped him.

"Alex, don't run off. I'm showing Allison the main building at Hidden Hills and we'll need your help getting Cherry there."

"I doubt she'll take my help." He glanced at the woman in question. "She's one of those independent women."

Tilda fought a grin. "You mean instead of one of those women who fall all over you." She glanced at

Allison, then back to him. "But then again, this one just might be one who stands up to you."

Alex started to leave when Allison made the trip back across the room. "Well, it looks like Mattie can handle every day but Wednesday afternoon." Those green eyes met his. "I'll just close the shop for those few hours." She smiled, and there was stirring in his gut and lower. "It looks like you've got an instructor for the class."

Tilda grinned. "That's wonderful." She hugged Allison. "You and Cherry have to stay for supper so we can celebrate. Before you argue, I already have a roast cooking. We'll show you the new community room where the classes will be held, and we need to go over a few details before I put everything up on the website."

They were all jolted back to reality as a child's cry rang out. "Cherry." Allison took off to the bedroom; Tilda followed close behind.

Alex went out to retrieve the child's wheelchair from the patio and carried it into the house. He pushed it down the hall just as Allison carried her daughter out of the bathroom.

When the girl saw him a shy smile appeared on her face. "Looks like I got here just in time," he said. "Your chair, *signorina*." He gestured toward the seat.

Allison hesitated, but her daughter leaned down, forcing her to place her there. Once she was secured in the chair, she looked up at him.

"It seems my daughter is a little smitten with you, Mr. Casali," Allison said.

"Since we'll be working together, it's Alex. And I will call you Allie."

That got a rise out of her. He found he liked to see her frazzled.

"I go by Allison."

"Tilda would like to show you around the guest ranch." He raised a hand. "Before you ask, it's wheelchair accessible, so Cherry can go along, too." He leaned down to the girl. "You want to go for a ride?"

The child nodded and looked at her mom.

"Yes, we can go," Allison told her.

They returned to the kitchen and found Tilda checking the roast in the oven. "By the time we get back supper should be done."

"I don't want to put you out, Tilda."

"Nonsense, like I said, we have to eat. And it's not often we get company." She looked at Alex. "This one lives like a hermit." She turned back to Allison. "Maybe you'll help change that."

Twenty minutes later, loaded into Alex's crew cab pickup, they took the mile-long trip to the guest ranch through a grove of trees. Just off the dirt road several log cabins came into view, then finally a large two-story structure appeared in the clearing.

"This is impressive," Allison said.

"Good." Tilda beamed. "There are twelve one- and two-bedroom cabins, and in the main house there are another ten guest rooms. We're advertising the main house for family reunions and business conferences and retreats."

Alex pulled into a gravel parking lot in front of the main house. "If you haven't guessed, Tilda is big on public relations," he said.

The older woman smacked his arm playfully. "Well, someone has to promote us. And you get top dollar for Casali Beef because I've advertised it online."

He adjusted his hat. "Word would have gotten around."

She huffed. "By that time I'd be in my grave."

Alex grumbled something as he climbed out of the truck. Allison didn't understand the language, but with the name Casali she figured it was Italian. How did an Italian end up in Texas?

The back door opened and Alex appeared to take Cherry out of the safety seat. "Come on, little one. Want to go for a ride?" He lifted her out of her seat and into the wheelchair.

Allison got out her side and hurried around the truck as Alex pushed Cherry up the ramp to the long porch. Tilda went on ahead and unlocked the double doors, then held them open. They walked into a huge room where the scent of fresh-cut wood teased her nose. Tilda turned on the lights and the massive room came to life. A large stone fireplace was the focal point. A wide staircase led to a balcony upstairs. A bar area took up another space along the wall. Furniture was still covered in plastic, but she knew it was leather. A rustic chandelier hung over a huge rectangular table with a dozen high-back chairs.

"This is amazing," she whispered.

"We think so," Tilda said, leading them toward the hallway and into another large room. "In here is where I planned to hold your class. It should handle twelve to fifteen tables and machines comfortably."

Allison looked around the room, checking the light coming through the window, measuring space in her head when she caught Cherry with Alex. They were at the windows, her chair close as he leaned over her, pointing to something outside. What interested her was the expression on her daughter's face.

"Allison, is there a problem?"

She turned back to Tilda. "No, I was thinking about all the supplies we're going to need, especially if there are beginners."

The older woman smiled. "Well, that's your department, and more money for you since you have the shop. I'll advertise for anyone who wants to attend, either bring your own supplies, or we'll make them available for an extra fee."

Allison finally smiled. "Are you sure people are going to attend?"

"I have a nearly filled class already. My goal is to get fifteen attending for the week. I love to quilt myself, when I have the time, but it's always been more about sharing the time with friends and family while creating memories."

"My grandmother taught me when I was about Cherry's age. Emmeline Cole was the talented one." Allison smiled at the memories. "I still have some of her quilts."

"See that's what I want to create with this retreat. Mothers and daughter together, making memories, and returning here year after year."

Alex watched Tilda and Allison from across the room. Maybe he should plan to go out of town while this retreat was going on. He looked out of the window, knowing they'd planned this guest ranch far enough away from the main house so not to disturb his operation or his privacy. But he had a feeling distance wasn't going to help him.

Keeping his distance from Allison Cole wasn't going to be easy. He glanced down at her precious child and felt a tug on his heart. There had to be more that could be done for her.

"Horsey?" she whispered as she pointed out of the window and off toward a mare and her foal in the pasture.

He tried not to act surprised on hearing her speak again. He knelt down. "That's Starlight and her baby." He smiled at her. "Maybe you can think of a name for him."

She looked up at him and those cornflower-blue eyes filled with wonder. She wrinkled her freckled nose, and he felt a strange protectiveness toward her. He couldn't help but wonder who had hurt this child so much that she didn't speak.

Tilda and Allison walked over. "What are you two up to?" Tilda asked.

Alex winked at Cherry. "It's a secret," he said as the girl became distant once again. He turned his attention to Allison and saw her hurt look.

He recalled a lot of bad years with a mother who'd lied and put herself before her sons. Allison Cole seemed to show real concern for her daughter. But people had fooled him before. People he trusted, who'd claim to love him, then walk away.

Now, he made sure people didn't get close enough to do any damage.

CHAPTER THREE

"YOU old son-of-a-buck," Alex called, trying to get control of the young stallion. The horse resisted the commands, kicking up his hind legs. Whiskey Chaser was having none of it, saddle or rider. Determination won out and Alex got the red dun calmed down and he finally fell into a rhythmic lope around the corral.

Alex felt little satisfaction since he'd been working non-stop the past week to saddle break the animal. He'd had too many distractions. Ever since Allison Cole and her daughter had arrived and disturbed his peace and quiet. Worse, he hated that he'd been watching for her to return to the ranch. That hadn't happened either.

He knew every detail of what was going on. Whether he'd asked or not, every night Tilda had filled him in on the progress with the retreat, and the opening was just days away. Great, people would be swarming the place, including the pretty mother and her daughter. A killer combination.

He walked Chaser back toward the barn and was greeted by his foreman, Brian Perkins. At forty, the one-time rancher and horse breeder had lost his own place through divorce. Ten years ago, he'd shown up at the ranch asking for a job. Back then Alex couldn't afford much, so Brian had cleaned stalls and herded cattle for a low salary and a roof over his head. He'd never complained about any task.

A few years ago, Alex had made him the foreman. It had been Brian who'd talked Alex into trying his hand with breeding and raising quarter horses.

"He did well today." Brian reached for the horse's reins, but Chaser whinnied and pulled away. "I still say you should put him on a track and see how he does. He wants to run."

"There's no reason you can't give it a try," Alex relented.

That was what he liked about Brian. The foreman threw out suggestions, but never pushed Alex into making decisions. Another thing he liked was that they never got too personal. He knew that Brian had been married, and had two kids, John and Lindsey, he supported. They'd visited him here in the summer. Other than that neither man shared much about their past. But Alex knew he could depend on Brian, same as Brian could depend on him.

Alex climbed off the horse as one of the ranch hands came out and began to walk him, cooling him down. He turned back to Brian when a vehicle caught his eye. He recognized Allison Cole's SUV right off. He followed the car's journey to the house, but she didn't get out. Instead Tilda came out, climbed into the passenger side and they took off toward the cabins.

"Looks like Tilda's about ready for the grand opening." Brian turned to him. "Are you?"

Alex pulled off his gloves. "No, I'm not crazy about the place being overrun by women."

Brian smiled, causing lines around his eyes. "I guess I'll stay clear of the place, too. I'll take my chances with the wannabe cowboys coming here in a few months. That should be fun."

Alex wasn't sure how any of this would work out. He wasn't too worried; he'd made bad investments before. It wouldn't break him, and, more important, it made Tilda happy.

"Have you got a crew together for the fall roundup? With the inexperienced riders, we're going to need extra help."

Brian nodded. "I have a feeling we're going to be doing a lot more of the work this year."

Alex looked toward the guest ranch. He wondered if little Cherry had come along today.

When he turned back, Brian was watching him. "It's a shame about the girl. Tilda told me how she reacted to Buckshot."

"Yeah, she was quite taken with him," Alex said, recalling the kid's excitement.

"You know, we have Maisie," the foreman suggested. "She might get a kick out of seeing her."

The pony had been included with some stock he'd bought at an auction. Alex found he wanted to see a smile on the little one's face, wouldn't mind getting a reaction from the mother, either.

"I guess it wouldn't hurt."

Allison pushed Cherry's chair into the conference room. She quickly counted sixteen tables. They were set up with sewing machines and a large table at the front of the room. She went to the oversized shelving unit lining one wall; it was filled with several bolts of fabric.

Tilda came up beside her. "I organized everything you ordered, plus the fabric you'd sent out from the shop. The shelves are labeled in decades, the 1920s, '30s and '40s fabrics." She pointed toward the other cabinet. "And here we have the quilt kits for the beginners. We have every supply you could need, too. If the women don't bring their own, there are rotary cutters, rulers, mats, seam rippers and thread." She looked at Allison and smiled. "Did I forget anything?"

"This is incredible, Tilda. You must have worked day and night to get all this done."

"I had help. Some of my friends from church came out. I sort of promised a few of them that they could sit in on the classes. They're such fans of yours, Allison. And they want to help with Cherry's care, too, and help you go around the class seeing who needs anything."

Allison couldn't believe this. The last two years had been a nightmare. It had been bad enough dealing with Cherry's condition, but her ex-husband had then stripped her of nearly everything, including her pride and confidence. It had taken a long time before she could be creative again.

"Oh, Tilda. This is an instructor's dream." She fought her emotions. "I can't thank you enough for all your help with this."

"Well, I advertised this as top of the line, and with your name that's what it will be." She smiled. "I just want you to be comfortable. I want to make this a twice-a-year event. We might be able to get you back on cable."

Allison froze. If she did that, Jack would get half the profit. He'd gotten enough already. No more. Besides, she meant to keep her promise to her daughter. "Let's start with this retreat first." She glanced down at her daughter. "With the shop and Cherry's therapy, I have a lot to deal with."

"Of course."

Suddenly Cherry began to make sounds as she pointed to the window.

Tilda leaned toward the child. "Well, would you look at that, Cherry? It seems Alex is bringing you another friend."

Allison watched the rancher ride in on his big black stallion, leading a gold-color pony behind him. She glanced down to see her daughter sit straighter in her chair. Even her expression changed.

"That's Maisie," Tilda told her. "She's been around for a few years. She's as docile as a big old dog, and she loves kids, not that we get many around here."

Allison watched as Alex climbed off his horse, tied the reins to the porch railing. Then he walked the pony away from the stallion and tied her to another post.

He glanced toward the window and tipped his hat, then he took those long, lazy strides back across the porch and into the building.

"That's one good-looking cowboy, even if he wasn't Texas born and bred," Tilda said.

Allison had to agree. Her heart raced with anticipation as she heard his boots on the wooden floor, and he appeared in the doorway.

"Afternoon, ladies," he said and strolled in as if he owned the place. Well, he did. He walked directly toward Cherry. "I have a surprise for you, *uccellino*." He pushed his hat back off his forehead, revealing his sandy-colored hair as his gray-eyed gaze met Allison's. "May I take your daughter outside to meet Maisie?"

How could she deny him? "Maybe we can all go along."

He nodded. "Let's go." Instead of taking the chair, he lifted Cherry into those big strong arms. Seeing the pleased looked on her daughter's face, she wasn't about to stop him, especially when she realized she was a little envious.

She and Tilda hurried along to keep up with Alex's long strides through the building and across the porch toward the golden pony with the white mane and tail.

"Cherry, meet Maisie. This pony has lived on the ranch for two years, but she doesn't have any kids to visit her. So she's pretty happy that you're here today."

Allison had to bite back her emotions as she watched her daughter lean forward and her tiny hand began to stroke the pony's coat. For the first time in a long time she felt hopeful.

Alex couldn't take his eyes off his charge. Something happened to him when she was around. Those big hopeful eyes, the sweet innocent scent of hers. Maybe she reminded him of himself and his brother. They'd been about Cherry's age when they'd been shipped off to America by a father who hadn't wanted them, to a mother who hadn't wanted them either.

He glanced at Allison. She seemed to care about her daughter, but why didn't the little one talk?

"Horsey?" the girl whispered so no one else could hear.

For some reason the child had chosen him to speak to. She trusted him with her secret. He wasn't going to betray her, yet.

"It's a pony, Cherry. Maisie is a pony."

Cherry gave him a shy smile. The word, "Pony," came as another whispered response. Then she leaned forward, trying to get onto the pony's back.

"Whoa, cowgirl," he said, pulling her back. "I don't

think you're ready for that yet. We need a saddle before you ride."

Allison came over. "Cherry, you don't know how to ride."

The child didn't like that and began to cry. Loudly.

Alex walked her away from the pony. "Crying isn't going to get you your way," he whispered in her ear. "Show your mom that you're a big girl."

Cherry hiccupped, and finally stopped. He pulled out a handkerchief and wiped her eyes. "Better? Now, today we pet the pony and maybe go riding another day. We have to get your mom's permission," he told her. "Okay?"

She turned those large eyes on him. He felt his heart melting and knew he was in trouble. He glanced over his shoulder, seeing the beautiful Allison Cole. Big trouble.

Two hours later, Allison and Cherry were seated at the kitchen table sharing another meal with Alex Casali and Tilda. She was surprised yet again when her daughter didn't balk about eating her food. Once Alex told her to finish her vegetables, and, although it was a slow process, Cherry did just that.

After supper Alex disappeared, leaving her with Tilda to discuss anything left to do before Thursday morning and when the retreat would open.

Tilda got out her list of things to do. "I only want you to worry about showing up. In fact, come the day before so you can get settled in your cabin."

"You know, Tilda, Cherry and I can stay in the main house."

"No, you need to get away from the others. I have a

feeling a lot of these women will be working on their quilts in the evenings. As long as you're available they'll monopolize your time."

"I guess you're right." She recalled her tours around the country at craft fairs. People wouldn't leave her alone even to eat. "I do need my time with Cherry." She glanced at her daughter, who had been looking through her books, but was now fast asleep.

"I think it's time I got her home."

Tilda smiled. "Oh, the little sweetheart. She's had a busy day."

Allison gathered her things. "I'll load the car, and come back to get her." She walked out of the back door into the dark night. After tossing her books on the seat, she went around to open the hatch for the chair. She started up the steps as Alex came out carrying Cherry. "You don't have to do that. I could have gotten her." It was a touching scene, seeing the big, gruff cowboy holding her baby.

"Well, I've got her, but I'd appreciate it if you'd open the door."

"Of course." She hurried back to the car and did as he asked. Alex carefully placed the sleeping child inside into her safety chair. Fastening the seat belt was a different story.

"Here, it's a little tricky." She leaned inside and immediately found how close the space was. She nearly collided with Alex when she turned his way. When their gazes locked her heart sped up as she felt his breath against her face.

"There, I got it." She quickly backed out. "I'll get the chair and we'll be out of your hair."

"Stay here, I'll bring it down."

Allison watched Alex climb the steps two at a time and went inside. Soon he returned with the chair folded and put it in the back of the car in no time. After closing the hatch, he came to her. "How do you lift that chair?"

"I'm stronger than I look."

He gave her a once-over and Allison could feel heat rush through her. "I have no doubt," he said. "But there's no reason why you can't take help now and then."

She glanced away. "I've found it safer to do it on my own."

He watched her awhile, then finally spoke. "I'll follow you into town." Before she could argue, he walked across the driveway and climbed into his truck.

She wanted to march over to him and give him her speech on how she didn't need help, especially from a stubborn, know-it-all cowboy. But the sun was setting, and she didn't particularly like going home in the dark.

Okay, she'd let him play hero this once, for Cherry.

Night had fallen twenty minutes later as Alex followed Allison's taillights past the city-limit sign. He turned in after her onto 2nd Street, the historical area of downtown. These storefront buildings had been around since the 1930s. She pulled into the alley at the back of her shop and parked. The area was dimly lit, only by the single bulb over the door. Great. Even though Kerry Springs was a good town, that didn't mean bad things couldn't happen here.

He pulled up behind her, then jumped out of the truck to get to the child, or Miss Do-It-All-By-Herself would refuse his help again.

He opened the car door and unbuckled the sleeping

child, then lifted her into his arms. The small girl curled trustingly against his chest.

He quickly shook the feelings away and followed Allison through the shop's back door. She paused to flick on a light, exposing a narrow hallway and a staircase. She turned to him as if she would take the child, but then instead she led him toward the stairs and they climbed up to a large open room that had once been an attic. The place was stifling hot. She went to the window and turned on an air conditioner.

"Cherry's room is this way."

She walked him past a bathroom and to a small room with a single bed. Allison tossed back the ruffled covering to expose white sheets.

He lowered the child to the mattress, but she opened her eyes, then started to fuss as Alex tried to step back. She grabbed onto him.

"Hey, it's okay. Let your mama get you dressed for bed and I'll come back to say goodnight." She continued to grip his arm. "Remember you're a big girl." When she finally let go, he glanced at Allison, then left.

He went down and took the wheelchair out of the car. After locking the car and back door, he carried the chair upstairs. He took his time to look around the makeshift apartment. It reminded him of one of the nicer places he'd lived in as a kid.

The large attic room had kitchen cabinets against one wall along with a small stove and, on the counter, a microwave. A sofa and chair with a bookcase and a small television took up the rest of the space. *Where the hell did Allison sleep? And why the hell were they living here?*

He turned away. Damn. He didn't want to see this place. How they lived. He didn't want any reminders of his past. It was time to get the hell out of here and forget about Allison Cole and her daughter.

Suddenly he heard his name whispered, and he turned to find Allison motioning him to the bedroom. The little girl was dressed in a nightgown and had a book in her hands. "I told Cherry you would read two pages and then she had to go to sleep."

He shouldn't have promised anything.

Allison stood in front of him and kept her voice low. "Look, you're the one who followed us home. Now, you have to take the consequences." She stared at him like a mother lion protecting her cub.

Alex walked into the room, sat down on the edge of the bed. "Show me where to start."

Cherry smiled and pointed to the exact line. It took all of five minutes before the child fell fast asleep. He put the book on the dresser and walked out.

Allison was waiting for him. "Thank you."

He only stared at her, then finally said, "Why are you living like this?" He pointed to the stairway. "And how long can you keep carrying your daughter up those steps?"

She straightened. "As long as I need to. Cherry's treatment has been expensive. So is starting up a new business."

"What about insurance?"

"There was a settlement after the accident, and I'm using that money for her therapy. We moved here because of her doctor. He's the best."

"What kind of accident?"

She glanced away. "Cherry was in the car when it was hit in bad weather."

Alex wondered about the details she left out. "Where's her father?"

Allison shook her head. "That doesn't matter."

"The hell it doesn't. It seems to me that both Cherry's parents should take responsibility for their daughter's welfare."

She shook her head. "Jack's out of our lives. I have full custody of my daughter, financially and emotionally."

Alex turned away. So her ex was a jerk. He knew all too well how easily a parent could walk away from their responsibilities. He looked at the small woman, stubborn and so determined to prove she could handle everything on her own.

He told himself to get the hell out of there; he didn't need this kind of headache. "Do you ride?"

She blinked at his question. "Excuse me."

"Have you ever ridden a horse?"

She shrugged. "Years ago."

"What about Cherry? Do you think she could sit in a saddle?"

Allison straightened. "I'm not sure that's a good idea."

"Did you see her today, how she responded to Maisie? You ever heard of horse therapy?"

"Yes, but I can't do anything until I ask the doctor."

"Then ask him," he said. "Because she's going to be at the ranch all next week." He took a step closer. "And another thing, your child is capable of talking. She's spoken three words to me. Today, she said, horsey and pony. It was barely a whisper, but she said them."

Tears filled Allison's eyes and something tightened in his chest.

"Hey, this isn't anything to cry about."

"I know. It's just been so long since I heard her speak. And she ends up talking to a stranger."

He couldn't help himself; he reached out and grasped her by the arms. Feeling her softness, he wanted so much more. "Sometimes it's easier to share things with strangers."

She looked up at him with those emerald eyes and, damn, if his throat didn't dry up as if he were a teenager.

A tear fell and he felt her tremble. "I just want to help her so badly."

He reached out and cupped her face, brushing a tear away with his thumb. "She knows that, Allie," he managed. "She'll come around."

Allison shook her head and pulled away. "No, she won't. I can't blame her, either."

"Why do you say that?"

"Because, I'm the one responsible for her accident."

CHAPTER FOUR

SHE was responsible for her daughter's accident.

Four hours later, Alex sat in his office at the house. It had always been his sanctuary, a place he'd come to work in peace and quiet after a long day. He'd chosen dark wood, with floor-to-ceiling bookcases filled with books on finance and business, many more on horse breeding. In his youth, he'd escaped into libraries to get out of the bad weather. That was when he had found he loved to read.

Thanks to Allison Cole's confession, there wasn't any relaxing with a book tonight. He went to the large picture window that overlooked the compound. Security lights lit the deserted area. He never should have followed her into town. Escorting her home had been the right thing to do, but it was staying and learning more about the woman that had been wrong. He didn't get close to people. He'd learned it was better to keep a distance, except for Angelo.

It was Cherry, he told himself. For some reason, the kid kept turning to him, pulling him into their lives. Probably because of that no-good father of hers. Tonight, Allison had mentioned the name Jack.

Earlier, Alex had done a search on the name Jack Cole. There were hundreds. He went to Allison Cole's website,

Quilt Allie, and discovered a Jack Hudson had been her business manager and, later, her husband. Most recently he had become her ex-husband. There had also been a list of items and books by Allison Cole for sale. Surely she would get any profit from the merchandise. Or did Hudson get the money and business while she got custody of her daughter? Was that how she had got rid of her ex?

Alex's hands fisted. He thought about his own father. He barely remembered the man, except for that day when Luca Casali had shipped him and his brother from their home in Italy to America.

At least Allison kept her daughter with her. He recalled the pain he saw on her face when she told him she'd caused the accident.

No way. Unless the woman was the best actress in the world, Allison Cole would lay down her life for her child. He walked back to the desk and turned on his computer. There had to be special saddles for disabled kids.

An email alert caught his attention and he clicked to see a list of personal messages. Angelo. He smiled, thinking about his famous pro-ballplayer brother. The New York Angel. Although now, their star was out for the season with an injury, and he was bored.

Alex wrote back that if he needed something to do, he could come to the ranch and work. At one time, his twin had been part owner in the operation. But Angelo hadn't wanted to be a rancher anymore than Alex wanted to be a ballplayer. They had invested in many other projects that had made them both wealthy men.

Then Alex opened an email dated over two months ago titled *Family Wedding*. He opened the saved message and began to read it again, already knowing the script off by heart.

Dear Alessandro,

Hello from Italy. I know it's been so long since you've heard from this side of your family, so I thought I would try to communicate with my long-lost cousins. Maybe the best way is to invite you to come to Italy and my wedding. It has been years and we're not getting any younger. I would love to see you both. Please, if you and Angelo would come, it would make my day perfect.

A formal invitation will arrive in the mail with the time and date.

Love, Lizzie.

Alex frowned as he reread the curt reply he had typed.

Lizzie,

Thank you for the invitation, but I have to decline. I'm too busy here to leave the ranch. Best wishes on your special day.

Alex

All of a sudden his father's family wanted him. Why was this happening after over thirty years? Where had they been when he and Angelo hadn't had a home or a family?

He shut off the computer. He didn't want to think of his family in Italy anymore. He wasn't about to ease their guilt. He wasn't the Casali who'd turned his back on the family.

Driving back from San Antonio, Allison glanced in the rear-view mirror at her daughter. Therapy hadn't gone well. Cherry had cried the whole time. Finally she'd had to leave the room while the physical therapist took Cherry through the exercises.

Allison pulled into the back of the shop, glad to be home. After retrieving the wheelchair, she lifted Cherry into it and pushed her through the back door. Hearing a man's voice coming from the front of the shop, she wheeled Cherry inside. The main room wasn't especially large, but it had enough space for everything for her business, materials, supplies and quilt patterns.

What she didn't have room for was a six-foot-three rancher. Alex Casali was dressed in his standard gear of jeans and a dark blue western-cut shirt that emphasized his broad shoulders. He should look out of place in the strictly feminine surrounding. Nope, he just looked all male.

She hadn't seen him since the night he had followed her back here. Not since she had poured out everything to him.

Allison quickly turned her attention to her part-time employee, Mattie. The older woman was actually giggling at whatever Alex had said to her.

She'd had enough of this. "Mattie."

The older woman swung around. "Oh, Allison, you're back already." She glanced down at Cherry as she walked toward them. "And you, little darling. You've had a rough morning, haven't you?"

Allison didn't take her eyes off Alex. "She had a difficult session today. She needs a nap. Why don't you take your lunch? I'll put Cherry down in back."

"Are you sure?"

Allison finally looked at the older woman. "Yes. And, Mattie, thank you for coming in early today."

The woman walked around the counter and got her purse. "It's never a problem, Allison." She looked at Alex. "It was good to meet you, Mr. Casali."

"The pleasure's mine, ma'am," he returned.

He watched the woman leave, then walked over to

Allison and gave a stern nod, then looked down at her daughter and smiled. "Hello, Cherry." The man was handsome, but now the transformation made him devastatingly so.

Even Alex Casali couldn't get any reaction from the child. "She's pretty tired."

But when she tried to turn the chair to leave, Cherry reached out for Alex. He didn't hesitate and lifted her into his arms.

"Sounds like you've had a busy morning, so you need to rest. But first, Maisie misses you. She wants to know when you're coming out to visit her again."

To Allison's shock, Cherry giggled.

Alex raised an eyebrow at the girl. "You don't believe she talked to me?"

Another giggle.

"Want to know something else? Maisie is ticklish. I'll show you where when you come to the ranch."

This time Cherry yawned.

Allison watched the exchange with envy. She stepped in. "I think this little girl is sleepy."

Cherry gave a weak protest, but went to her mother. Allison carried her to a small backroom that was an office. It also had a daybed. She placed Cherry on the mattress and pulled a lightweight blanket over her. Her eyelids were drooping, and finally closed.

"Sleep tight, sweetie." Allison kissed her, then walked out.

Alex took a walk around the shop. The old storefront was far from fancy, but everything was organized in rows of bins and up on shelves. Along the high walls were several colorful quilts. He examined them closely, realizing that Allison Cole was a talented woman. Okay, maybe he could understand why Tilda wanted her for the retreat.

Alex went to the large worktable. On top were several cut squares of cloth, stacked in neat piles. Some were sewn together. He glanced at an oversized notebook that read "Patterns." He opened it to see drawings of different shapes on the paper. One was labeled "Wedding Wishes", the next page "A Sister's Bond." He continued to the next one, "My Cherry's Delight."

He glanced up to see Allison and tried not to act as if he was doing anything wrong. "She asleep?"

Allison walked over to him. "Yes." She closed the book. "Is there something I can help you with?"

He shook his head. "I'm here to help you. To take out any supplies you need for the retreat."

She blinked. "I don't want to put you out. I'll just bring it all out tomorrow with us."

"If you were putting me out, I'd tell you. I was in town anyway."

She nodded. "Thank you. I do have two bins packed up. They're on the landing."

He continued to stand there. It was hard not to notice her striking looks. She had large emerald eyes, a creamy complexion and a sweet kissable mouth. Her hair was tied back in a ponytail, showing off her delicate jaw line. His gut tightened in need.

She looked away. "Well, if there isn't anything else, I don't want to keep you."

"As a matter of fact there is. Did you ask the doctor about Cherry going riding?"

She shook her head. "No, but I did discuss it with the therapist. She says horse therapy might be good for

Cherry as long as she uses a special saddle, and only if she wants to do it."

"I got the saddle." He saw her shock. "I guess we'll see if she really wants to ride when you come out tomorrow."

"Wait, you bought a saddle for her?"

He shrugged. "Not a big deal."

"It is to me. Saddles are expensive, and a special-needs saddle has got to cost a fortune."

"Don't worry about it, Allie. I'm not going to go hungry. Not anymore."

The next day, Allison walked into the place she and Cherry would call home for the next week. Within a group of tall trees was the new two-bedroom cabin. It had a spacious main room with a huge stone fireplace, and an open kitchen with Shaker-style cabinets and dark granite counter tops. The best feature was the hardwood floors throughout.

"How do you like it?"

She turned around and saw Tilda in the doorway. "It's amazing. I could live here forever."

Tilda's eyes lit up. "Maybe we could work something out."

Before Allison could respond, the woman went outside. Allison followed her to get Cherry. Off the deck was a ramp that connected to a concrete walkway that went all the way to the main building. That meant she didn't have to struggle with Cherry's chair.

"Thank you for adding the walkway and ramp."

Tilda picked up another box from the back and smiled. "You're welcome, but it was Alex who thought about it. So thank him."

Allison was confused. She hadn't thought he wanted

her here. Instead he'd bought a saddle so Cherry could ride, and now this. Don't you turn out to be a nice guy, Alex Casali. Then he'd really be too hard to ignore.

She went to the back to get Cherry. "Come see our new house, sweetie." She lifted her out of her safety seat, but when she turned away from the car she nearly ran into Alex.

"Oh, sorry. I expected Tilda."

"She had to take a phone call, another reservation. Here, let me carry her."

She didn't argue when he reached for Cherry; she couldn't stop the gasp when his fingers brushed against her breast. The contact sent a tingle across her skin, catching her off-guard. She quickly moved away, then went to get the chair already on the porch and followed them inside.

"Hello, *uccellino*," he said to Cherry.

Allison found she was a little jealous of the attention that Alex gave so freely to her daughter. And it was crazy. Technically he was her employer. And she needed this job.

Inside, Alex placed Cherry in her chair. "So what do you want to do today?"

Cherry looked at her mom, giving her a hopeful look. Of course her daughter wanted to see the horses. "Maybe you need to tell me," Allison coaxed.

Cherry frowned in frustration, then she looked at Alex for help.

Alex was surprised that Allison was pushing her daughter. He looked at the little girl. "Your mother's right." He reached for the child's hand. "Tell me like you did before, Cherry. I know you can do it."

The girl gave him a stubborn look, reminding him of her mother. Those blue eyes challenged him.

"I guess you won't see your surprise today," Alex told her.

She glared harder, then leaned toward him and finally whispered, "Horsey."

Allison gasped at the single word.

"Good job, kid. And maybe if your mom says it's okay, then you can go riding on Maisie."

Allison nodded. "After lunch and a short nap."

Alex stood. "Okay, then I'll be back when you wake up." He was rewarded with a smile from both of them. He needed to get out of there. "See you later."

Before he could get away, Allison called to him as he stepped off the porch landing. He turned around to the woman in jeans and a T-shirt. Her hair was pulled back into a sloppy ponytail and she wore no makeup. She still took his breath away.

"What is it?"

She shrugged. "Just curious as to what you call Cherry in Italian?"

"*Uccellino*. It means little bird."

She smiled. "That's sweet."

He snorted. "I've been called a lot of things in my life, but never that."

She smiled and her eyes slanted upward. "I think your secret is safe." She grew serious. "Thank you for getting Cherry to talk. You have no idea how much it means to me."

A funny feeling centered in Alex's chest. He wasn't sure he did, but he was quickly realizing what her praise did to him.

That same afternoon, Allison sat on the corral fence and watched the big smile on Cherry's face. She was so proud of herself riding on Maisie. She sat secure in the saddle with a padded back brace and a strap cinched securely around her waist. A ranch hand led the pony around the arena, while Alex walked next to her, coaxing and praising the tiny rider.

"She's doing really well."

Allison swung around to find a man who looked to be in his early forties. He had an easy smile and kind hazel eyes. "Yes, she is."

"I'm Brian Perkins, Alex's foreman."

"Allison Cole." She smiled. "I'm working the quilting retreat this week."

"I know." He nodded. "And that's your daughter, Cherry."

They both watched as Alex stopped and instructed Cherry. "I never thought I'd see the day," Brian began. "A female having her way with the boss."

The foreman's words were pretty telling. Allison didn't doubt that Alex Casali kept pretty closed up. He had his own way, and she couldn't help but wonder why.

But she craved privacy, so she owed him the same. She didn't need to get personally involved with this man. Any and all men were off her list.

"She's a charmer, all right," Brian said. "Reminds me of my girl at that age. They seem to learn early on how to work us poor males."

"Oh, really? Excuse me while I get my violin out. Poor males? I don't think so."

Brian began to laugh, and she soon followed and didn't notice Alex was walking toward them.

"If you have time to stand around, I guess I don't give you enough to do."

They turned to see Alex. He didn't look happy.

The two men exchanged a long look, then Brian turned to Allison. "It was nice to meet you, Ms. Cole."

"It's Allison," she corrected. "And it was nice meeting you, too, Brian."

The foreman walked off toward the barn and Allison turned back to the angry-looking Alex. "Is there a problem with me talking to Brian?"

"None that I know of."

"I have one. You were rude."

"I run a large operation here. My only concern is that everyone does their job."

Allison smiled at her daughter seated on the pony. "If Brian Perkins is your foreman, I suspect he works hard at his job."

Alex hated that she could read him so easily. He had no reason to care if Brian was flirting with her. But he did. "Everyone who works for me does, but I pay them well." He glanced toward the barn and saw Jake bring out another horse. "How about we forget about my foreman and you show your daughter you can ride, too?"

She shook her head. "Oh, no. I haven't been on a horse since I was about ten years old."

"Good, you have some experience." The ranch hand arrived. "Jake, this is Ms. Cole. She and her daughter, Cherry, will be around here for the next week."

The young cowboy tipped his hat. "My pleasure, ma'am." He smiled at the girl. "It's nice to meet you, too, Miss Cherry. I'm Jake."

The girl smiled shyly.

Alex handed over Maisie's reins to Jake. "Here, you hold onto Miss Cherry while I get her mother settled on Honey."

"Sure thing, boss," Jake said.

Alex took Allison by the arm and walked toward the saddled horse. "Honey is as gentle as they come."

"I can see that, but I don't appreciate not being asked first."

He stopped next to the mare. "I did ask. The day at your apartment."

She jammed her hands on her hips. "You asked if I had ever rode a horse. You never asked about me about riding today."

Silently Alex counted to ten. The woman was going to drive him crazy. "Okay, would you like to ride today?" He raised a hand. "And before you answer, look over there at your daughter's face."

They both turned and saw a smiling Cherry.

"That is so unfair," she said. "Using my child to get what you want."

"No, I am trying to get Cherry what she wants." He grabbed Honey's reins and brought them back to the saddle. "Now, are you going to disappoint her?"

She wrinkled that cute nose. "Never."

He reached for the straw cowboy hat that was hooked on the saddle horn and placed it on her head. "Then let's get started. It's left foot in the stirrup."

Allison brushed back the wayward strands of hair and grabbed the reins from him. "Forget that. Just give me a boost up."

What was she up to? He finally did as she asked and locked his fingers together. She placed her sneaker-covered foot on his hands and pushed upward onto Honey's back, giving him a view of her well-shaped bottom. A short view, because she was upright in the saddle in no time. She slipped her feet into the stirrups, and tugged on the reins, causing the horse to back up.

She pressed her hat down, then with a click of her tongue the horse shot off toward the far end of the corral. At the fence, Allison turned Honey around, then kicked the horse's sides and together they shot off in a full gallop back to him.

A smiling Cherry was clapping her hands as she watched the goings-on.

Allison tugged on the reins and came to a stop in front of him. Her antics brought whistles and cheers from the men who stopped to watch her.

"You're just full of surprises, Allison Cole."

She shrugged. "I guess I didn't forget as much as I thought."

He realized that he would be the one finding it hard to forget her.

CHAPTER FIVE

THE next morning Alex stood at his office window and watched as several cars drove down the road, heading toward the guest ranch. It was opening day for the Quilters' Retreat and there would be a couple dozen women here, invading his space. His privacy. He hoped he hadn't made a mistake on this.

His thoughts turned to Allison and Cherry. Just a short time ago he hadn't known mother and daughter existed. Now, it seemed they'd pushed their way into his life and he hadn't had a thing to say about it, or a way to stop it.

Over the past couple of days he'd been around the woman and her child more than he needed. Between the horseback riding, and getting them settled in the cabin, they'd shared space and time that had disturbed his routine and peace of mind.

He shut his eyes. He could still see Allison staring up at him with those large eyes, when she got that stubborn look, telling him she had to do it herself. Fine, she could do it all by herself.

He wasn't about to let the woman tie him up in knots, but the child was a different story. Whether

Allison knew it or not, she needed help with Cherry. She couldn't do it all on her own. Was he the one to help her? And if he tried would she accept help? Probably not.

Alex grumbled as he turned around to the desk and found Brian standing in the doorway. "I called out to you, but you seemed to be thinking about something else."

Alex ignored the comment. "Do you need something?"

The foreman stepped further into the room. "The guy from Gilbert Ranch is here to pick up the bull. I need the paperwork."

Alex had forgotten all about it. "It's on the desk."

Brian found the bill of sale, but didn't leave. Instead, he came up beside Alex and glanced out of the picture window.

"So today is Tilda's big opening."

"Yeah, she's been running around like crazy getting everything ready."

"I know, the boys have been moving a bunch of boxes over there the past few days." He sent a quick glance toward Alex. "I don't think they mind helping out, especially for Allison."

"What do you mean?" Alex turned to him. "They better not be bothering her."

Brian shrugged. "I'm sure Joey and Pete flirted a little, but they're pretty harmless. They're respectful."

He tensed. "Make sure they don't hang out over there. Allison has a job to do, and so do they."

Brian frowned. "Come on, Alex, you know Joey and Pete. They're good kids, but you have to admit Allison Cole is a pretty distraction."

Alex drew a breath. "I still don't want them bothering her."

"You're mighty protective. Why don't you just admit that you're attracted to her?"

"Allison Cole is an employee at the ranch for the next week. Besides, she's not my type."

Brian raised an eyebrow. "Allison is every man's type." He snapped his fingers. "That's right, you don't get seriously involved."

Alex sent him another glare. "Look who's talking."

"Hey, at least I gave marriage a shot," Brian said. "Besides, I can't afford a woman. My kids will be going off to college in a few years."

Alex turned his focus back to the scene outside the window. "You don't have to worry. You'll have enough." He walked to his file cabinet, opened the top drawer and pulled out a file labeled Perkins. He handed it to Brian.

"I opened an account the second year when the ranch started making money. I took part of the profits and gave it to Angelo to invest. My brother's not only a good ball-player, he's good at making money. If it weren't for the bad market the last few years, there would be more."

Brian opened the file and swore. "Alex, I can't take this."

"Why the hell not?" he grumbled. "You worked as hard as I did to build this place. Consider it a bonus."

Brian stared down at the account's huge balance and shook his head. "I can't tell you how much I appreciate this. It was rough not being able to be a full-time father to John and Lindsey, but now I can give them what they need without any worries. Thank you, Alex."

Alex envied his foreman for his family. "From where I stand you did a good job with them. You never abandoned them. So don't let anyone ever tell you you aren't a good father."

Alex thought about Allison again. How could a man give her up? And their child? He didn't have to search further than his own father for the answer. Luca Casali hadn't batted an eyelid when he had put his three-year-old twin sons on an airplane and allowed them to fly off to a strange country that was not only an ocean apart, but worlds apart.

Brian interrupted his thoughts. "That little Cherry is hard to resist." He turned to Alex. "She seems to have gotten pretty attached to you."

Alex didn't want that. He couldn't let anyone get close to him. Only his brother. He'd learned a long time ago, it was safer just to keep his distance.

Allison glanced up at the clock and saw it was nearly five. Where had the day gone? Since it had taken most of the morning to get everyone set up in class, they hadn't really gotten down to work until after lunch. She'd quickly learned that most of these women weren't amateur. She liked that, knowing serious quilters would finish their projects and be ready to go to the long-arm quilter by the end of class.

Allison stood and walked around the tables, noting that the women were well under way. She stopped and commented on choices of fabrics and patterns. She even helped a beginner student choose material for their projects. The women ranged from the early twenties into their seventies. There were two sets of mothers and daughters, Trudy and Sally Monroe, and Connie and Alissa Huntington.

She glanced toward the bank of windows and saw her own daughter sitting there with her favorite doll, but she wasn't playing. Instead she was looking through the glass toward the ranch. No doubt she was searching for Alex Casali. The cowboy had been scarce today.

She hated the fact that his recent disappearance bothered her. She kept thinking about how he'd treated Cherry. The attention Alex had given her child. A child starved for a father. That was the main reason she couldn't let her daughter get too attached to him. After this was over she'd move back into town, and there'd be no more horses, or brooding cowboys.

Besides, she wasn't too trusting of men these days after her own disastrous marriage. Jack had been handsome, attentive at first, but in the end he hadn't been there for them. As a father, he'd been worse. He finally admitted he'd never wanted kids.

No. No matter how handsome Alex Casali was, getting involved would be a bad idea.

"Allison."

She turned around to see Jenny Collins, a thirty-something, single teacher from San Antonio. She was a beginning quilter. "Yes, Jenny."

The teacher smiled proudly. "I just wanted to show you my points. Are they okay?"

Allison examined the block of machine-stitched fabrics where the triangle points were sewn together on her pinwheel pattern. To an expert's eyes the points were just a fraction off. "This is wonderful. You've done a great job with your first project." Allison picked up a pair of scissors and demonstrated how to clip the back side of the fabric.

Jenny nodded, and then suddenly glanced across the room. "Oh, my, will he be joining our class?"

Allison turned around and Alex was standing in the doorway. His presence alone was overwhelming with his height and broad shoulders that filled the entrance.

"Oh, no, that's Alex Casali, Tilda's partner in the guest ranch."

The teacher's smile brightened even more. "Maybe I should have signed up for riding lessons."

Allison, too, admired the handsome rancher, then soon realized that he was disturbing her class. "I doubt that Mr. Casali gives riding lessons, but you could ask him."

Allison walked over. "Alex, is there something I can do for you?"

"I thought your class would be over by now." He glanced toward the window, then back to her. Those gray eyes locked on hers. "I thought Cherry could go for a ride."

She felt her heart accelerate at the thought of spending time with him. "Well, I'm not exactly finished here. It's going to be a longer day than I thought. It was nice of you to ask, but I can't get away."

"I could take her myself," he offered.

Allison looked at her daughter. Cherry had spotted Alex and her face lit up like a neon light. Without any hesitation, Alex started across the room and she hurried to catch up with him. She wanted to stop him, but, seeing her daughter's response, she couldn't do it.

"Well, hello there, little one. How was your day?"

Her doll forgotten, Cherry reached out and grabbed for Alex's hand.

"Has she been stuck in here all day?" he asked.

Allison reared back. "No, we had lunch at the cabin, and she's been outside. Tilda's friends, Carol and Charlotte, have been with her."

Alex ignored her again. "Well, she needs exercise. How about I take her riding on Maisie?"

"I told you I can't get away right now."

"I can take her now, and you come later."

Allison wanted to have this discussion alone, but there wasn't any way that would happen with nearly twenty women in the room. She turned and noticed most of the class had abandoned their work and were watching them. "Okay, you can take her, but only walk her around the corral."

He started to reach for Cherry's wheelchair, but Allison touched his arm. "We need to discuss this later," she said, her voice low and controlled. "So we don't have any misunderstandings in the future."

His jaw tensed as he stared at her, then he nodded and gripped the handles on the chair. "Let's go, *uccellino*. Maisie has been waiting all day for you to come by."

All Allison could do was watch as they left. She turned back to her class. "It's officially quitting time, but since we got started late today, we could work a little while longer. I want to make sure everyone is off and going on their projects."

Tilda walked up to her. "I appreciate this, Allison. Don't worry, Cherry is in good hands."

Allison nodded. That was what she was afraid of.

Later that evening, Allison eased the door to Cherry's bedroom shut. She was finally asleep. Her daughter had been keyed up since her ride with Alex, but it seemed to take that kind of exhaustion to put her to sleep.

Allison went to the kitchen table and began to look over tomorrow's lesson. She'd learned today the different levels of the students attending her class. Everyone wanted her to demonstrate something, from her hand-stitched appliqués, to her patterns and color sugges-tions. She'd loved every minute of it. It had been a long time since she felt this focused on anything but Cherry and she was excited about tomorrow.

There was a knock on the door. She went to open it and found Alex, with hat in hand, standing on the small porch. He looked as if he'd showered and shaved. Was he going out?

She shook away any thoughts of his personal life. "Alex, is something wrong?"

"You tell me. You summoned me here."

She tried not to be intimidated, but it was difficult. "I just want you to give me a little more warning about riding, instead of barging into my class."

He watched her a moment. "Just tell me what kind of jerk you were married to?"

Allison blinked, and then quickly closed the door behind her as she stepped onto the porch. "Would you keep your voice down? And who I was married to is none of your business."

"It is when you look at me as if I'm the devil himself. I would never do anything to hurt that child, and I'm tired of trying to prove that to you."

He started to walk off when she reached for him. "Alex, please, you're right. I haven't been fair to you." She sighed. "It's just that I've been overprotective of my daughter ever since the accident."

Alex knew he should keep going. *Walk away. Don't get involved in her problems.* "Is that because it was your fault?"

In the dim porch light, he could see her pain and sadness.

"I wasn't driving the car, but I wasn't the mother that I should have been."

He cursed. "I can't believe that."

She shook her head. "It's true. I was working all the time. As the show climbed in the ratings, I was spending more and more time away from Cherry. Then it seemed I was always busy designing new quilting patterns while my three-year-old daughter was being cared for by nannies."

"What about your husband?" He found it was hard to get the words out. "Shouldn't he take responsibility in this, too?"

She turned away.

He came up behind her. Seeing those delicate shoulders held so rigidly, he ached to reach out and touch her, to pull her back against him, to absorb her burden. "Allison…"

She turned back and looked up at him. "Jack didn't want children. When I got pregnant, he wasn't happy. Since he was also my manager, he thought it would ruin my career. Instead it brought in more viewers. Jack used that and made a deal to extend my show to an hour."

"What about Cherry?"

"In the beginning, I had her close by, even on the show at first. But as she got older, things changed. I couldn't have her on the set because she was distracting. That's when Jack hired a nanny."

"What did you want?" Alex asked.

"To take some time off to spend with my daughter, just do the show on the Internet at my own pace." Her eyes were glossy with tears. "I lost my own mother and dad at an early age. I wanted my daughter to have hers. I didn't think that was too much to ask."

Alex tried to remain calm, but seeing Allison upset made it difficult. "It wasn't. So why didn't you do it?"

"I was under contract, and Jack said I couldn't change anything, or I'd have to give back a lot of money. He convinced me to hang in for another year, and we'd renegotiate the contract. Eleven months later, Cherry was with her nanny when their car was rear-ended by a drunk driver."

He reached out and wrapped Allison in a tight embrace. Her softness made contact with his chest and he closed his eyes, reveling in it. Dear Lord, he couldn't remember feeling anything like this. He cupped the back of her head and felt her tears against his shirt.

"Allie, believe me, Cherry's accident wasn't your fault."

He thought back to his own mother. How she'd neglected both him and Angelo. How she had ignored them, blaming them for the fact that Luca had never come for her.

Alex drew back, but refused to release his hold on her. "Cherry survived, Allie. She's getting better, every day."

"Why won't she talk to me?"

"She will, and I expect it'll happen soon."

"Really?" she whispered.

"Really." He leaned closer, allowing her sweet breath to caress his face. He watched as her eyes widened, not out of fear, but desire.

"Alex…" She spoke his name on a breathy whisper.

"Damn, woman, you're making this hard."

Alex pulled her closer. That was his first mistake. The second was when he lowered his head to hers. He paused, his eyes searching hers, wanting her to put a stop to this craziness. When she didn't reject his advances, he captured her mouth. At first he just enjoyed the feel and taste of her. He released a groan of need, wanting more.

His gut tightened as she pressed against his body. He went to work on her sweet mouth, angling one way then the other to get more of her. His tongue sought entrance and she opened with a whimpering sound that nearly drove him over the edge. With the last of his resolve, he tore his mouth away and gasped for some air for his starved lungs.

He caught her surprised gaze, knowing she felt it, too. This wasn't good. "I've got to get out of here."

He turned to leave, but she reached for him. "Alex."

Alex stopped and looked over his shoulder. "Don't push this, Allie. I don't think either one of us can handle the consequences."

With that, he walked off the porch, knowing he'd kill for just another taste of her. He couldn't let that happen. He couldn't let anyone get that close.

CHAPTER SIX

"CHERRY, stop crying or you aren't going riding tomorrow."

The next afternoon, Allison loaded her daughter into the car for her therapy session. As usual she was putting up a fight. She didn't like having to leave the ranch. This struggle upset them both, but in times like this a parent had to take charge.

Slowly the crying died into a quiet sob. Allison closed her eyes and released a tired breath, trying to push away the feeling of helplessness. After a second or two, she pulled herself together and turned the key but, instead of the engine coming to life, she heard a clicking sound.

She tried again. Nothing. She sent up a silent prayer and tried a third time. All she heard was Cherry starting to fuss again in the warm car. "It's okay, honey."

Then there was a knock on the window. She gasped and turned to see Alex. He pulled open the door and leaned forward. "What's wrong?"

Since their kiss last night, she'd been hoping not to deal with him so soon, but now she didn't have any choice. "I think my battery is dead."

He glanced toward the backseat. "Hi, Cherry."

Her daughter giggled.

Alex turned back to Allison; those eyes pierced hers. "Let's get her out of the hot car."

She ignored the sensation he stirred in her.

He walked around the back and lifted the hatch to get the wheelchair. He was at the side door and unbuckling Cherry before Allison could get it together.

He lifted her child out. "You're getting pretty heavy, little one. I think you're eating too much," he teased her as he sat her in the chair. Then he reached into the car and unlatched the safety seat.

"What are you doing?" she asked.

"I'm driving you and Cherry to therapy." He raised an eyebrow. "You have a problem with that?"

Allison wanted to refuse his offer, but she couldn't. Even if there hadn't been much progress, Cherry needed these sessions. It was her only chance to walk again.

She nodded. "Thank you, I'd appreciate it."

He blinked. "That's a surprise. I thought for sure I'd get an argument."

"Not when it comes to my daughter."

Thirty minutes later, they arrived at the medical building in San Antonio. Alex planned to sit in the waiting area, but Cherry began to fuss, so he went along with her.

He wasn't happy about how the child was manipulating everyone to get what she wanted. Okay, she was hard to resist, but she also knew how to work them all.

The therapist came into the large training room. With a smile she walked up to Cherry. "Hello, Cherry." She looked at Allison. "Hello, Ms. Cole." Then to Alex. "You must be Mr. Cole."

Allison stiffened. "No, Kate, this is Mr. Casali. He drove us here today. Alex, this is Kate Boyer, Cherry's therapist."

He nodded. "Miss Boyer."

Kate looked him over, then glanced down at Cherry. "If we're lucky, Cherry might want to show you what she's been doing." Kate pushed the wheelchair to the other side of the room. "Have a seat, Mr. Casali."

"Alex."

The young therapist's smile grew. "Kate."

When he took a seat, Allison sat beside him in the row of chairs. He watched the therapist go through a series of exercises, and then ask Allison if they'd been doing them at home. Alex saw her uneasiness as she answered, "Sometimes."

He liked Kate's no-nonsense approach. She wouldn't let the child's tears or stubbornness sway her as the workout continued. But with every attempt, the therapist would praise her efforts. Then toward the end of the session, Kate whispered something to the child. With a nod, she motioned for him to come over.

"I think Cherry wants to show you something," Kate said. "This is her first attempt, but since she seems to be responding today, she's willing to try." Kate looked at Allison. "It's the parallel bars."

Allison tensed. Every time they'd even suggested it before her daughter had had a meltdown. "I thought we decided to wait."

Kate glanced at Alex. "I believe there's someone here she might want to impress."

Allison was wondering if Kate wanted to impress Alex, too. Oh, God, was she jealous?

Kate's eyebrow rose in question. "Two months

ago, Dr. Meyers wanted us to work with Cherry wearing braces."

With Allison's nod, the therapist strapped the braces on Cherry's tiny legs. Then she wheeled her over to the parallel bars and locked the chair into position. With the help of another therapist, Cherry got to her feet. Allison saw her daughter's panic and wanted to put a stop to it.

She felt Alex's hand on her shoulders. "Hold on. She can do this."

"Oh, Alex, she's so little."

She saw a flash of compassion in those steely gray eyes. "And because you love her and want her to get well again, you need to push her."

Allison bit down on her trembling lip and nodded.

He rewarded her with a hint of a smile, and she felt her heart tighten. He released her shoulder and they turned back to Cherry, who now was standing.

"Well, would you look at you, *uccellino*." He beamed at her as he made his way to the bar. "Now let's see what you can do."

Allison saw her daughter's panicked look, but let Alex handle it. She stood at the end of the bar as he coaxed her. The therapist helped move her tiny legs. A tear fell from Cherry's eye and down her cheek, but she kept going. After four hard, grueling steps, Alex swept the child up into his arms and hugged her tightly.

"I'm so proud of you," he said as he brought Cherry to Allison. "And you know who else is proud? Your mom."

To Allison's surprise her daughter reached for her. She gladly took the burden. "I love you, Cherry. You did such a good job." She held her daughter for a long time, then realized that Cherry's weight plus the braces was heavy.

Kate removed the extra hardware and settled Cherry back into her chair. She hugged her patient goodbye and waved as they left.

"I think we need to celebrate." Alex pushed the chair toward the elevators. "I'm taking you lovely ladies out to dinner and it's Cherry's choice."

Two hours later, after an hour at a children's pizza place, Alex managed to get Cherry and her mother home. He waited in the cabin's living room for Allison to put the girl to bed.

Why? Why was he waiting? He didn't need this at all. He'd already stepped into Allison Cole's business, and now he was involved in the girl's therapy. He felt a tug in his chest remembering the child taking those steps, seeing her pain, but she wouldn't quit. He paced to the door and back. Leave. Keep your distance, he told himself, but still he wasn't listening.

He turned as Allison walked from the hall. She looked tired, too. But those eyes locked with his, and he saw the mirrored awareness.

"Now that she's asleep, I should go."

She didn't answer, just kept coming toward him. Her eyes were filled with emotion, determination in her step as if she was on a mission.

"Please, not before I thank you."

"There's no need." He found himself backing up, but the door stopped his progress.

"Do you have any idea how many months we've worked to get Cherry to try and stand?" She blinked her beautiful eyes as she teared up. "She would never do it until today, until you asked her."

Hell, he didn't want to be the kid's hero, but it looked

as if he had the job. "Hey, I'm also the one who has the horses, and your daughter is drawn to them." And he was drawn to her mother. He reached out and brushed the moisture away. Her skin was so soft. He wanted to touch her everywhere. He quickly shook away that thought. "So we use whatever we can to get her to work on her therapy."

"Why?" she whispered. "You never wanted us here."

Hell, if he knew. "I'm a private man, but Cherry is just a kid. She's gotten a raw deal, so if I can help…" he shrugged "…why not?"

"I appreciate that. But I can't ask you to come to every one of her therapy sessions."

"You didn't ask, I'm volunteering." Was he crazy? Yes. The mother-daughter duo had gotten to him.

For a long time Allison just stared at him, then walked away.

"What's wrong?" he asked.

She swung around to face him. "I don't know if that's a good idea, Alex. What happens when we leave here? When she doesn't get to come here every day to ride?"

"Then bring her out. If I'm not around, one of the hands can help her. I'll make sure of that."

She still didn't look satisfied. "What about what happened last night? Between us."

"I thought that was mutual."

"I can't start up anything." Her gaze darted away. "I don't know if I'll be able to…again."

Hell, he wanted to pound the guy who'd hurt her. "There's no worry about that. But I'd be lying if I said I wasn't attracted to you. As you are to me."

"But we can't do anything about it."

He was annoyed that she could brush it away so

easily. There was a lot they could do about it. For a short time anyway.

She looked up, but her gaze didn't meet his. "You have the ranch, Alex, and I have my shop and Cherry—"

She never got to finish her denial as he captured those sweet lips with his, sending a surge of heat through him. With a groan, he wrapped his arms around her shapely body and pulled her against him. His hands moved over her, wanting to feel every inch of her. Brand her with the taste and feel of him so she would never think about another man.

But, damn, if she wasn't doing exactly that to him. He tore his mouth away before he lost it altogether.

She gasped for air, but didn't pull back. He wanted her, bad. "You're probably right—it isn't a good idea."

He released her and opened the door, feeling the cooler air, but it didn't help him. When it came to Allison Cole, he doubted anything could.

The next day passed quickly as Allison stayed busy so she wouldn't think about Alex. It didn't work. The man was interfering in every corner of her workday.

"Ladies, class is finished for today, but, as before, you're all welcome to keep working on your projects."

A few of the women stood up, walked around and went to get water and coffee. That was what she needed: caffeine. She hadn't slept much last night, not after Alex's kiss. Even knowing that getting involved with the man was crazy, and harmful to her daughter, she couldn't control her attraction to Alex.

She checked her watch and knew that Cherry was riding Maisie. What would it hurt for her to take a short ride, too?

* * *

Alex was walking Maisie when he saw Allison come out of the barn leading Honey. She had on snug jeans and fitted pink blouse that highlighted her glorious red hair. Covering her head was the hat he'd given her the other day, but the surprise was the buckskin boots on her feet.

She looked as if she belonged on a ranch.

"Mommy," Cherry whispered.

He felt a smile coming. "That's right, little girl. That's your mommy." Sexy mommy, he thought. He was still hot and bothered over the kiss they'd shared last night. He also knew he should keep his distance from this woman.

"So the teacher's playing hooky."

Allison went to her daughter. "No, this teacher is finished for the day. Hi, sweetie," she said to the girl. "I thought I'd come riding with you."

Her idea got a smile from Cherry. Alex felt the excitement, too, but refused to show it.

"It's not very exciting riding around the corral." He finally caught her gaze. That was a mistake. "But we could go to a creek not far from here."

Allison sobered, as if thinking it over. "How far?"

"About a half-mile," he told her, and then turned back to Cherry. "I guess we should reward our girl here for her hard work yesterday."

"Maybe we should," Allison agreed.

Alex pulled a ranch hand aside and gave him instructions to saddle his horse, and then he called Tilda on his cell to let her know where they were headed.

He closed his phone and turned back to Allison. "It's always good to let someone know where you are."

She smiled. "And Tilda worries about you."

He grumbled under his breath. "I've taken care of myself far too long to need anyone worrying about me."

Half an hour later, Allison was enjoying their ride through the beautiful hill country. Tall oak trees lined the path, filtering the late afternoon sun. She caught sight of a whitetail deer off in the thick foliage. She glanced ahead to see that Cherry, seated on Maisie, was pointing to the animal, too. Beside her daughter was Alex gripping the pony's reins as he led the way on a gelding named Wild Bill.

They both kept a close eye on Cherry, but she seemed to be able to sit in the saddle just fine. Allison had noticed, just in the few times her daughter had been on the pony, she'd gained strength in her back and posture. If this was what it took to get the child to improve, she would bring her out to the ranch every day to ride.

How would Alex Casali feel about that?

Allison knew that wouldn't be a good idea. She needed to stay clear of the man, before she ended up hurt again. Cherry was the catch. Her daughter was so taken with the handsome cowboy. It seemed both mother and daughter had the same problem.

Suddenly she heard the sound of water as they rode through a clearing and the wide creek appeared before them. Large rocks and boulders ran along either side. Ancient oak trees arched over the water's edge forming a canopy.

"This is so beautiful."

Alex climbed down. "It's one of many creeks on this ranch." He began to untie his blanket from the saddle. "But Lucky Creek is one of my favorites."

Allison got off her horse and went to Cherry. She wasn't sure if they were staying or not until Alex spread the blanket on level ground.

"Come on, *uccellino*. You want something to eat?"

When Cherry gave him a big nod, he worked the safety straps and lifted her off the pony, then carried her to the blanket. He set her down gently, then went back to get a bag.

Allison sat beside her daughter, then glanced across the creek and saw another deer. "Look, Cherry, there's another deer."

Although her daughter didn't react as strongly as she had with Alex, she saw the excitement in her eyes. That gave her some hope.

Alex handed her a canvas bag. "What's this?" she asked.

"Something Tilda threw together for us – it pays to let her know where we're going. I guess she didn't want us to starve out here in the wilderness." He turned to Cherry. "So we're having a picnic." He poked his finger into the child's middle causing her to giggle.

Alex looked at Allison and saw the hurt. She tried to hide it, but she couldn't. "How about if your mom looks inside and sees what we've got to eat?"

Allison pulled out containers of sandwiches, potato chips, fruit salad and bottles of tea and juice. "Boy, did you luck out. There isn't a vegetable to be found."

Cherry giggled as her mother opened the containers. The girl chose a peanut-butter sandwich, leaving ham and turkey.

In between bites, Alex told them stories about the ranch. Things that Tilda had told him since the land had been in her family so long.

"Do you know why they call the creek Lucky?" Alex asked.

Cherry shook her head.

"Well," Alex drawled. "There are a few stories out there. One is that the water makes a big turn," he said as he pointed downstream. "It's almost in the shape of a horseshoe. And we all know horseshoes are lucky."

Allison finished her sandwich. "What's the other?"

"A long time ago, I believe it was in the nineteen hundreds, there was a big flood in this area. Tilda's grandfather was a boy. He'd gotten too close to the edge and fell into the rushing water."

He caught the wide-eyed look in Allison's eyes.

"How did he get out?" she asked.

"Well, that's the mystery. It seems he was headed downstream when he landed on a sandbar out in the middle, then he caught onto a branch of these big oak trees and just hung on tight. Soon help arrived, someone tossed him a rope and pulled him to shore." He nodded. "And that's why they call it Lucky Creek."

He glanced down at Cherry, who was leaning against her mom sound asleep. "Seems I bored my audience."

With Alex's help, Allison shifted her daughter into a more comfortable position, but kept her close. "She's had a busy day."

"So have you," he told her, but didn't move away. "What made you decide to ride?"

"After sitting all day, I needed to move around." Her eyes met his. "I didn't think there was a problem with me riding."

"There isn't any that I can think of."

"Good." She stood and walked toward the water.

He followed her. "As long as that's all it is."

"What else could it be?"

"This attraction between us. This itch I feel for you and you feel for me."

She started to deny it, but he placed a finger against her lips. "At least let's be honest, Allie, especially when you're standing there looking so hot and bothered that you couldn't even sit beside me."

She blinked at that and backed up. "Well, that's no better than you saying you want nothing to do with me, then kissing the daylights out of me before you walk out."

"Hey, if you want to carry this further, I'm willing."

"You are the most egotistical man I've ever met."

"No, I'm just honest." He leaned forward. "I can tell how you've been turning me inside out. I haven't had a decent night's sleep since I laid eyes on you. Like now, when your green eyes turn all smoky and your voice gets breathy."

She tried to glance away, but he cupped her face, making her look at him. "Now, it's your turn to be truthful."

"I can't, Alex. I can't let this happen."

"It's already happening, Allie." His mouth closed over hers and after a moment of resistance she melted against him. Her surrender frightened him more, but he wasn't listening to the warnings as he felt a sizzle of heat when he parted her lips with his tongue. She sighed a murmur or moan, he wasn't quite sure over the pounding in his ears as he took the kiss deeper. His hands moved over her back, then down to her bottom, drawing her to him.

He tore his mouth away, trailing kisses along her jaw, her neck, to feel her shiver. He returned to her mouth, angling one way and another, hungry for more, needing her as he had never wanted anyone.

His hands went to her breasts, cupping her through her blouse, but he needed to feel her skin. He tugged her shirt from her jeans and made contact with her heated flesh.

"Oh, Alex," she whispered in a breathy plea, causing a passion in him he'd never known. Her hands were on him, working to free his shirt from his jeans.

He did the job himself as the sound of the popping snaps suddenly made him aware of what was happening, and how they were getting out of control, but didn't care. That was when he heard the sound of the vehicle.

He hugged Allison close against him and released a breath. "As much as it kills me to stop, someone's coming.

With a gasp, she turned around and worked quickly to pull herself together. He squinted into the dusk falling as he looked toward the dirt road to see Brian's truck.

After tucking in his shirt, he checked to see Cherry was still asleep, and then walked to the road. One of his ranch hands got out of the truck. "Jake," he greeted. "Is there a problem?"

"I'm sorry, Alex." The kid glanced over at Allison. "Brian sent me out here. He tried your cell first, but he got your voice mail."

"Okay, you gonna tell me why you're here?" he asked, knowing it better be good.

"It's Cheyenne Sky. She's having trouble with her foal. Brian called the vet, but he thought you would want to know."

Alex released a breath. They'd been watching the prize brood mare. "Yeah, I want to know." He turned as Allison walked over. "One of my brood mares is in trouble."

"Then you need to go," she told him.

"Okay. We'll take the truck," he told Jake. "Can you manage the horses?"

With a nod from the ranch hand, Alex went and gently lifted Cherry into his arms and instructed Allison to get in the seat of the crew cab truck and placed her daughter on her lap. Then with a wave to Jake they headed back.

Once back at the guest cabin, Alex carried Cherry inside and into her room, placing her on the twin bed.

Then he walked out and stood in the living room.

Man, he felt as nervous as a teenager, wanting to be with his steady girlfriend. He'd never had a steady girl ever. Never wanted one. And here at the age of thirty-eight, he was panting after Allison Cole.

In the past he'd always been able to keep his distance from women. He hadn't felt this vulnerable since he was a kid. He didn't like that. Not at all, but he wasn't ready to give her up.

He looked up as she walked out of the bedroom; her fiery hair was mussed and her green eyes still deep with desire. Unable to resist, he crossed the room and raised his hand to cup her face.

"This isn't over, Allie." Then he kissed her thoroughly to make sure she would lie awake thinking about him. He wanted to brand her so she wouldn't forget him. When he finally broke it off, she didn't look any happier than he felt. Good.

CHAPTER SEVEN

THE next afternoon, Allison finished up the class session a little early, hoping to see about fixing her car. Something she'd totally forgotten about during the past twenty-four hours.

Her thoughts went to Alex as they had so many other times in the two weeks since they met. She'd let herself be distracted by him. So much so she had lain awake last night for hours, thinking about his kisses, how his hands felt on her skin, setting her on fire. She'd finally had to get out of bed and begin work on a new quilt pattern.

She had three more days here, which meant she had to figure out a way to be around the man without turning into putty whenever he looked at her. Well, it had been easy today since she hadn't seen him at all.

She was nearly out of the door when Jenny stopped her to look at her quilt. The young teacher had been working on the traditional Wedding Ring pattern using lovely pastel colors and subtle prints.

"Oh, Jenny, I can't believe you've nearly finished," Allison said, happy at how well the class was going.

Jenny shrugged. "There isn't much nightlife and only reruns on television."

"But still, you must have been up half the night."

The pretty blonde beamed. "I wanted to get it finished before I start back to teaching." She sighed. "As much as I enjoyed this class, I may come back here when the dude ranch opens over Christmas vacation." She smiled. "I wouldn't mind passing time over the holidays with a good-looking cowboy. And what better way than coming to a ranch?" She frowned. "Of course, I'm finding that most of the ranch hands aren't much older than some of my students."

"That's true, but it can still be fun," Allison agreed. She had a feeling Jenny was looking for more than a good time. "If you do come back, drop by my shop in town and see me."

Jenny nodded, but was distracted by something outside. "Oh, my. I hope he's going to be one of the cowboys."

Allison looked toward the porch and saw Brian standing by her car. "That's Brian Perkins, the ranch foreman."

"He's handsome in a rugged sort of way." She gasped. "Please don't tell me he's married."

Smiling, Allison shook her head. "From what Tilda told me, he's been divorced for years and has two teenage kids. And they're a big part of his life."

Jenny grinned. "I teach teenagers. I love them."

"How interesting." Allison had an idea. "Come with me—I need to ask him about my car so I'll introduce you."

Allison had only an hour of free time since Tilda and one of her friends were watching Cherry. She needed to get a new battery before the therapy session tomorrow.

When she went outside, Brian greeted her with a tip of his hat. "Hello, Allison."

"Hi, Brian. This is one of my students, Jenny Collins."

Brian gave another salute. "A pleasure to meet you, Jenny."

"Nice to meet you, too, Brian."

Allison saw a flash of interest in Brian's eyes before he turned back to her. "I didn't want to interrupt class, but I need to let you know that your car is running again."

"Oh, Brian, you didn't need to do that. Was it the battery?"

He nodded. "I replaced it this morning, and it starts just fine."

"Thank you. How much do I owe you?"

He shook his head. "Alex took care of it."

She stiffened. The man seemed to take care of everything whether she liked it or not. "Well, then you can give him my money."

The foreman held up his hands. "Maybe you should talk to him yourself."

"Okay, where is he?"

"In his office at the house."

"I'll go see him, then." She wasn't going to let him continue doing this. She turned to Jenny. "Would you let Tilda know where I went?"

With Jenny's nod, Allison left the couple on the porch, got into her car and headed to the ranch house. She was going to let Alex Casali know that he couldn't have everything his way.

Inside the back door, Allison called to Alex, but when he didn't answer she headed down the hall in search of his office. She couldn't help but look at the beautiful surroundings. Each room she passed had been profession-

ally decorated in rich green and brown tones, some too
dark for her taste, but everything was tastefully done.
The hardwood floors gleamed under plush area rugs.
Every inch of woodwork had been perfectly restored,
and a marble fireplace took the spot of the main focus
in the large living room. The one thing it was void of
was photos. There wasn't a single family picture
anywhere.

She turned and continued to another doorway and
glanced inside. Floor-to-ceiling bookcases filled two of
the walls, and a huge oak desk sat in the middle of the
room. Behind it was a large bay window that overlooked the ranch.

As she peered further into the room she found Alex
in a high-back leather chair. Sound asleep. He didn't
look nearly as hard, or as intimidating, or as Italian as
his name stated. His sandy-brown hair was mussed,
falling across his forehead. He had long black lashes,
high cheekbones, and a nose that was a little crooked.
His jaw was shadowed by a day's growth of beard.
There was a faint scar beside his right eye. Yet none of
it took away from his good looks.

She felt her heart race as she continued to survey his
broad chest and wide shoulders, right down to his narrow
waist and long legs encased in a pair of worn jeans.

She blew out a breath as her gaze went to his hands.
Large with long, tapered fingers. She shivered, recalling his hand on her body last night. Getting involved
with this man would be a mistake. A big one, but she
was afraid it might be too late to heed the warning.

Allison started to turn away when he said her name
in a husky voice that caused a warmth to spread through
her. When their eyes met, she immediately felt the in-

tensity of his gaze. She couldn't even manage a word as she walked toward him.

"I'm sorry to disturb you," she managed. "You probably didn't get any sleep last night. How's your mare?"

"She's fine now, after finally giving birth to one stubborn chestnut filly."

She smiled. "That's nice. Maybe I can see her. I mean I'll bring Cherry by—if it's okay with you."

"Any time." He stood and she backed away. "Can't say I blame you, I probably smell like a barn."

He smelled just fine. The real reason was she didn't trust herself. "You're fine."

He walked to the window, raking his fingers through his hair. She wanted to go to him, touch him, run her hands over his broad back, recalling the feel of his muscular body against hers.

No! She glanced away from temptation toward his orderly desk that held a computer screen. On the glass top was what looked like a wedding invitation. She wasn't trying to read it, but she did notice it wasn't written in English.

"It's my long-lost cousin's wedding invitation."

She jumped at the sound of his voice. "I apologize. I didn't mean to read your mail. I just noticed it's in Italian?"

With a nod, Alex leaned against the window frame. He wasn't in the mood to share this with her, with anyone. "My so-called family lives there."

She smiled at him. "How nice. Are you going?"

Why did she have to look so good today? Alex wondered. He'd thought about her during his long night coaxing his mare through a rough delivery.

He glanced away. "As far as I'm concerned I don't have any family except my brother."

She nodded.

"Was there something else you needed from me?" he asked. "I haven't been to bed yet. So unless you're offering to go there with me, I'd like to end this visit."

He saw the hurt in those jade eyes, and for the first time in a very long time he felt like a heel. But it was for her own good. She turned and walked out. He could handle the love-hate thing, just not the happily ever after. Whether she admitted it or not, Allison Cole wanted just that. He suddenly wished he could be the man to give it to her.

The next afternoon, Allison was surprised to find Alex waiting for her when she pushed Cherry outside to her car. Dressed in dark jeans and a starched blue shirt, he looked so good. She suddenly was rethinking her resolve to give up on men. How crazy was she?

"Well, good afternoon, Cherry girl," he said, making her daughter grin. He stood and took possession of the wheelchair.

She managed to find her voice. "I wasn't sure you were coming today."

"Why? I promised I'd help."

They headed toward his truck. "Yes, you did, but—"

"If I give my word," he interrupted, "I keep it."

"Fine. It's your time." She turned her attention to Alex's backseat where she was surprised again to see a new safety seat. She refused to mention it. If he wanted to go with Cherry to therapy, who was she to deny her daughter the help?

Thirty minutes later they arrived at the center and immediately Kate jumped into another strenuous routine for Cherry. Both she and Alex stayed close by, encouraging and coaxing her all the time. Even when the tears came, Alex just kept on making deals with the child to keep her going on.

When the session ended, Alex placed Cherry in her chair. The girl looked exhausted as she drank water.

Kate also came over. "You did a wonderful job today, Cherry. I'm so proud of you." The therapist looked at Allison. "Dr. Myers would like to talk to you if you have a few minutes."

"I'll stay with Cherry," Alex offered.

Allison nodded and stood. "Thanks. I'll be right back."

Once alone, Alex pushed the wheelchair over to a bench where he sat down. He turned Cherry around to face him. "*Uccellino*, it's time you stop this game."

The pretty blonde child didn't look at him.

"You're a big girl now, Cherry Cole. It's time to start talking to your mom."

She finally raised those wide baby blues and he felt a hard tug on his heart.

"We both know you can. So why not speak to her?"

A tear rolled down her cheek. "She'll go away," she whispered.

At first, he was relieved to hear her tiny voice, then he realized her panic was the same as he'd felt as a child himself. Those times when he had sat alone, scared his own mother would never come back. He pushed away the memory. Allison wasn't anything like Cindy Casali. He brushed at her tears. "Oh, little one, your mother would never leave you."

The child nodded. "She did before." Another tear, then another. "I want her to stay with me."

It all came clear to him. As long as Cherry refused to get better, she'd have her mom's full attention.

"You're wrong. She isn't going to leave you, ever. I promise. But you'll never know unless you start talking to her."

Then the girl glanced away.

"You're going to be five soon. Don't you want to go to school and have friends?"

She turned back to him. "I want us to live with you and Tilda at the ranch."

His chest tightened as he realized how much this little girl had added to his life. How much he wished there had been someone in his life to make time for him.

"Oh, sweetheart. You know you're always welcome at the ranch." He lifted her into his lap as her tiny arms circled his neck. Another barrier came crashing down and Alex didn't know if he could handle letting either one of them go.

The next evening, Allison finally finished up her class for the day. Earlier Tilda had taken Cherry back to the ranch house for supper so she wouldn't have to hang around and wait for her mother.

She was planning on sharing the evening meal with the women when she looked up and saw Alex standing in the doorway of the room. She paused and admired the handsome rancher in the black jeans, a burgundy western shirt, and shiny black boots. Dear Lord, she'd never seen a man look so good.

"Allison." He nodded. "I have a message from Tilda."

"Has something happened to Cherry?"

"She's fine. Tilda just wants to know if it's okay if she spends the night?"

Her daughter wanted a sleepover? "Oh, that's so much trouble."

"I don't think Tilda feels that way about Cherry. I have no doubt she's enjoying every minute of it."

Since the accident, Allison had always worried about leaving her daughter with anyone. "What about Cherry?"

"They were both working on a jigsaw puzzle when I left."

She was a little sad that she would be alone tonight. "That's good. I want her to be independent." Allison gave him a brave smile. "Thanks for letting me know."

He pulled out his cell phone and pushed a button, then placed it against his ear. "Tilda. Yeah, she said it was okay." He nodded and held out the phone to her. "Your daughter wants to talk to you."

Allison's heart stopped suddenly as Alex handed her the phone. "Cherry?"

"Mommy," came out in a tiny whisper.

"Oh, honey," she managed as tears flooded her eyes. "Do you really want to stay all night?"

"Yeah."

Every soft word spoken caused her such joy, she could barely speak. She wanted nothing more than to run over there and hug her daughter, but didn't want to overwhelm her. "Okay, I'll see you in the morning. I love you."

"Love you, too. 'Night."

"Goodnight, sweetie." She handed the phone back to Alex. "Thank you."

"Why are you thanking me? I didn't do anything."

"Okay, play tough guy, but I'm not buying it. You somehow convinced my daughter to talk again."

He shrugged. "Maybe." His steely gray eyes met hers and she felt a different kind of emotion. "Go to dinner with me, and I'll tell you my tricks."

Allison knew Alex Casali had a lot of them. One of them was making her fall head over heels for him. "Will you give me a few minutes to clean up?"

After his nod, she turned back to the women in the room who were all smiling. She let them know she wouldn't be staying after all, but would be here the first thing in the morning to answer any questions. She turned to leave, ignoring several comments about her sexy cowboy. She knew one thing for sure. She couldn't ignore her feelings for Alex any longer.

An hour later, Alex walked Allison into a small family-owned Mexican restaurant in Kerry Springs. An older couple greeted them with a warm smile.

"Alessandro, it's been a long time," the older woman said, giving him a big hug. The heavy-set woman in her fifties had black hair laced with gray pulled back into a bun.

They exchanged words in Spanish, and then Alex turned to her. "Juan and Maria, this is Allison Cole. She owns the Blind Stitch shop downtown."

A smiling Maria grasped her hands. "So good to meet you, Allison." Then she looked back at Alex. *"Muy bonita."*

"Sí, bonita."

Allison found herself blushing. *"Gracias,"* she said.

Juan stepped in. "Mama, our guests are hungry," he said. He led them through the dimly lit restaurant out to a terracotta-tiled patio edged with small trees adorned with tiny lights. They were seated at a wrought-iron table in a secluded corner. "Enjoy."

Mr. Lopez left them alone. "They are a lovely couple," Allison said.

He glanced across the table at her. "They're probably saying the same thing about us."

Allison couldn't look away from his penetrating gaze. Did he want them to be a couple? No, she couldn't go there. "I bet the food here is good," she said.

He raised an eyebrow. "I think so, but you tell me." He motioned for the waiter and they ordered dinner.

When the wine arrived, she took a sip, hoping it would help her relax. "This is very good."

He nodded. "I'm glad you like it. I don't drink much. My mother did far too much."

"I'm sorry." She released her glass. "I'm not much of a drinker, either. This is the first since Cherry's accident. It's the first time I've gone out."

Alex watched her expression change. "Hey, don't go getting sad on me. You should be happy—your daughter is speaking."

Her pretty face broke into a grin. "She is. And I have you to thank for that."

He shrugged. "Cherry would have talked eventually, but she's pretty stubborn." He took a drink of his wine. "A lot like her mother."

Her happiness seemed to fade. "Is that the reason she hasn't talked? She's angry at me?"

"Cherry isn't angry." She stared at him as he toyed with his glass. "She's afraid you'll leave her."

Allison's eyes widened. "How could she think that?"

"She told me if she got better, you'd leave her again, like last time."

"Damn Jack for all his lies."

Alex reached for her hand and gripped it tightly. "It's okay, Allison."

"No, it's not. I allowed my husband to run my life. He kept me from my own child. Worse, I let him."

He hoped he never ran into the guy. "Well, you're doing it right now. So put the past aside, and move on. Cherry's improving every day. Her therapy's going well. She'll be walking one day."

Allison looked up at him with those beautiful jade eyes. "You think so?"

His gut tightened. "I know so."

She quickly brushed away a tear and smiled. "Oh, Alex, be careful. You're turning into a nice guy."

He doubted that.

"And that makes you hard to resist."

He grinned at her. "That's my plan."

Two hours had gone by way too quickly as they walked out of the restaurant. After no lack of conversation during their meal, they suddenly grew silent during the ride back to the ranch. Alex enjoyed the quiet. He always had. The full moon overhead lit the road, adding to the intimacy. Finally he pulled up in front of the cabin as he had many other times, but tonight Cherry wasn't in the backseat. Selfish as it was, he wanted time alone with her mother.

He got out, went around to the passenger door and lifted Allison down. When her slim body made contact with his, he couldn't resist. He lowered his head and kissed her because he couldn't wait any longer for the taste of her, the feel of her against him.

When he finally tore his mouth away, they were both breathless. "Allie." He rested his forehead against hers. "You're driving me crazy."

Allison suddenly realized they were outside in front

of the cabin silhouetted by the porch light. What was he doing to her?

"It would probably be wiser if I said goodnight right here before I get into trouble," he warned her.

Disappointed, she started to step away, but he drew her close to his side and walked her inside the dimly lit cabin. Her heart raced as he pushed her back against the closed door and kissed her as if it were their last time. "I'm not very wise when it comes to you."

She wrapped her arms around his neck, pulled him down and kissed him again. "I guess I'm not either."

His gaze bore into hers. "It would be crazy to take this any further."

It was her turn. She had the choice to send him away, or have the man stay and make love to her. "Yeah, crazy," she breathed.

He closed his eyes. "I've never wanted a woman as badly as I want you."

Allison felt the same as she placed her mouth against his, sending another surge of heat through her. He groaned and wrapped his arms around her body and pulled her against him, deepening the kiss. She let him.

Alex swung her up into his arms and headed down the hall into the master bedroom. The king-size bed took center stage. The rich cocoa-brown comforter was masculine, but there were some feminine touches, too, including satin sheets.

He stood her on the floor, then turned her around to face him. His finger touched her jaw, tilting her face up to his. "Tell me to walk out that door."

Allison felt her body turn hot, her breasts grow heavy. With a moment of unexpected and reckless desire, she couldn't move and realized she didn't want to. He saw her hesitation.

"Not so sure?"

"No!" she denied, then her voice softened. "It's just I haven't been with—"

"Anyone but your husband," he finished.

She nodded.

He released her with a curse. "Look, Allie, this isn't going to work. So let's put a stop to it now."

Before she could find her voice, he'd turned and headed out.

She tried to call him back, but he didn't stop. Then she heard the cabin door close and she was suddenly alone. She curled up on the bed, telling herself it was probably best he had left. But if that were true, why did she feel more alone than she'd ever felt in her life?

CHAPTER EIGHT

At five the next morning, Alex drove up to the house. He climbed out into the cool predawn air, glad there was no one else stirring, yet. He knew work had already started on the ranch, but he wasn't ready for the daily routine. Not yet.

He'd been driving around most of the night, trying not to think. Not to see the hurt look on Allison's face before he had walked out on her. But he knew if he'd stayed he could never leave her. He wasn't ready for that. She wasn't either.

He walked inside the house. Relieved to find the kitchen empty, he started upstairs to his bedroom. Stripping off his shirt as he went, he entered the moss-green room with dark furniture and a king-size bed.

Everything was big and masculine. Not a thing was feminine. Why would it be since there had never been a woman in here? That was the way he wanted it.

Dropping his shirt in the hamper, he went into the connecting bathroom and turned on the water in the shower. He removed the rest of his clothes and stepped inside the stall, then let the warm water begin to work its magic. He closed his eyes, and once again Allison Cole appeared in his head.

Just hours ago, he'd stood beside her bed. She had been willing. Her fiery hair draped against her shoulders, her mouth swollen from his kisses. Her body pressed against his.

Alex groaned as a strange feeling stirred in his chest. Damn, if he never wanted any more than to climb into bed with her. Make love to her and then again. The honest truth was he knew he'd never get enough of her.

He opened his eyes and grabbed the soap to wash away any thoughts of spending more time with her. He'd already broken too many rules. Number one, he'd spent entirely too much time with her, making him feel things he hadn't felt in a long time. He didn't like that. He stepped under the spray of water, trying to rinse away the soap along with all the memories of a woman who had burrowed in a lot deeper than he'd ever allowed anyone. If he let her, she might find her way into his heart. Deep down, he knew it was already too late.

It was six-thirty when Allison walked up the steps to Alex's house. She was feeling confused and insecure. God, Alex was the last person she wanted to see and he certainly didn't want to see her. But no matter that she'd been relieved nothing had happened between them, his rejection still hurt.

The sound of her child's laughter pushed aside everything else. She put on a smile and went inside. Cherry was sitting at the table as Tilda worked at the stove, singing a silly song. Her daughter was clapping her hands and Allison's heart soared. For the first time in a very long time she had hope that things would get better.

Tilda looked at her. "Well, look who's here. Good morning, Allison."

"'Morning, Tilda, Cherry," Allison greeted as she went to her daughter and kissed her. "So, did you have a good night?"

Her daughter nodded. "I did a puzzle."

Allison bit her lower lip. "How fun. What else did you do?"

Cherry glanced at Tilda. "Go on, tell your mother."

"I stayed up late." Her pretty blue eyes sparkled. "'Cause I did my exercises."

Another miracle. "That's wonderful. I'm so proud of you."

Her daughter's smile widened. "And I get to ride Maisie, too."

"Good. Today is my last day of class. Then you and I are going to be spending a lot more time together. Does that sound like a good idea?"

Her daughter nodded as Tilda carried food to the table. "I've set you a place, and if you go get Alex we can eat."

Allison would rather walk over hot coals. She stood up. "Where is he?"

"In the office."

Allison went off down the hall. All she had to do was call to him. Besides, if he wanted nothing to do with her all she had to do was get through today, and tomorrow they'd move back to town. And she could forget ever knowing the man. That appeared to be the way he wanted it.

Alex stood at the window, his phone next to his ear, listening to his brother complain about a shoulder injury that had sidelined the future Hall of Fame pitcher for the season.

"You could come stay at the ranch if you're bored."

"Thanks, Alex, but if I want to work, it won't be around smelly cows and horses."

Alex grinned. "Is the only reason you called me to complain?"

"Oh, man, I almost forgot. Did you get the email from Isabella? There are a few surprises. She sent wedding pictures."

Alex went to his desk and turned on the computer. He found the email and clicked on it.

Since you couldn't be here for the special day, I'm sending along a family picture. Cristiano couldn't make it either, but I thought I would attach his picture anyway so you can get a glimpse of all of your family that are very eager to meet you, perhaps one day soon...

The photo appeared of the large group enjoying Lizzie's wedding, and Alex began to search for anyone familiar. Then he clicked on the separate photograph attached to the email.

"Oh, sh… Who is he?"

"Cristiano Casali," Angelo said. "He's our half-brother."

Alex continued to stare at the young man who looked remarkably like him and his twin. Then his attention went slowly back to the man in the back row of the wedding shot, Luca Casali. The man who hadn't had room in his life for his sons, so had just sent them away. Had he ever regretted it? Had he ever thought about them? Suddenly emotions clogged his throat. "I've got to go, Angelo. I'll call you later."

Alex hung up, but he kept looking at the photos. All the years of pain and loneliness hit him hard. Lost in his past, he suddenly heard his name. Standing in the morning light, he saw Allison. She looked pretty dressed in her trim trousers and white blouse. His heart raced and he felt a stirring in his body that he didn't need right now.

"Allison."

"I'm supposed to tell you breakfast is ready."

All at once he felt a need for her. He got up, went to her and drew her in his arms, then captured her mouth in an eager kiss. After he pulled back, he said, "Now that's a better way to start the morning."

She still didn't smile.

"You're angry with me because I had to leave you."

She shook her head and stepped back. "You were right, it would have been bad to take our relationship any further. Since after today, when class ends, you don't have to worry about running into me. We only have to make it through breakfast."

She started to leave, but he grabbed her by the wrist, stopping her. "You think that's why I left you, Allie?"

She closed her eyes. "Don't call me that."

He leaned closer. "You didn't mind last night."

She shook her head. "Stop it," she breathed. "You walked away from me last night. I don't know how I'm supposed to act, Alex."

Hell, he didn't know how to act either. He wasn't supposed to feel like this about her. She wasn't supposed to get this close. "I left because you weren't ready for what little I could offer you."

"Did I ask for anything more?"

"Your type always wants more." When she tried to pull away, he held tight. "You deserve more."

He dipped his head and nibbled on her mouth. "But

if you're willing to settle I've got some ideas on how to spend a few hours."

She pulled back. "Not a good idea."

He agreed. "So we agree to stay away from any more trouble." He gave her a quick kiss. "Now, let's go get some breakfast." Reluctantly, he released her and went back to turn off his computer.

Allison followed him and saw the pictures. "What a lovely picture. Family?"

He nodded. "You could say they're family. They live in Italy."

Allison stared down at the large group. "You're lucky. I lost all of mine."

"You're welcome to mine."

She didn't miss the sarcasm in his voice as her gaze combed over each person, eager to know Alex better. She stopped as she saw the smaller photo of a younger version of Alex. "Is this your twin brother?"

He shook his head. "No. I believe that's my half-brother. Seems my father remarried and had another family to replace the one he shipped off."

Allison watched the pain flicker across his face. "So your mother took care of you."

"When she wasn't drinking or on drugs. The only thing Cindy ever wanted was for Luca Casali to come after her. Instead she got stuck with a couple of kids and died trying to drink away her misery."

Allison gasped. "Oh, Alex, you can't mean that."

He glanced at her, his eyes dark with anger. "At least after she died, we stopped hoping she would get clean and want us."

How could a mother not want her children? "She had a problem."

"Stop whitewashing it. If our mother had cared, she wouldn't have left two kids alone all night, or forget to feed us; she'd worry that we didn't have heat or water to bathe, or that we were living on the street. As far as Angelo and I are concerned, our mother didn't even try. No one tried."

Allison's heart went out to him. She didn't have the words to help him deal with the anguish. "You still have a family in Italy and your father is alive. Maybe you could reconnect with him now."

"That's almost funny since Luca has only contacted us once in all these years."

"Maybe there were reasons." She moved closer. "Maybe you owe it to yourself to find out."

Later that afternoon, Allison was wrapping up her class and saying goodbye to her students. She'd felt good about everything she'd accomplished on her first retreat. Several of the women had already talked about returning for her next class. Honestly, she wasn't sure she'd be back to do another one.

If she hadn't gotten so close with Alex it might be different. He'd told her that he didn't get involved long term. She wasn't about to be a convenience. She deserved more. Besides, Cherry had to be her main focus. Although she'd made such great progress, there was a long way to go.

So why was her day clouded with worry about Alex? The turmoil he had to be going through over his family. What a horrible life he and his brother must have had growing up. Her heart went out to them both.

A commotion at the door caused her to turn around to see Tilda bringing in several ranch hands to help the guests load up their things. After directing them to their tasks, Tilda walked over to Allison.

"I didn't think I'd feel this sad now that it's over." The older woman hugged her. "Thanks to you, Allison, the retreat was a great success. Any time you want to do another one, please let me know. In fact, a few of the women were asking how you felt about doing a class at your shop."

Allison thought eventually she would like to do that. "I'm not sure if I have the room where I am at right now, but I might be able to swing it two times a month, if the group stays small enough."

"Or we could meet here," Tilda added. "You and Cherry can continue to stay in one of the cabins."

That would heighten her chances of seeing Alex. "I'm not sure that's a good idea. It's a long drive from town."

"You can have it on a day Cherry comes to go riding."

Allison had forgotten about the riding. How would Alex feel about her coming back every week? "I'm not sure it's a good idea."

Tilda studied her awhile. "Look, I may be getting old, but my eyesight is still pretty good. Whatever has happened between you and Alex is your business. Just so you know, in the ten years I've known Alex Casali, he's never acted this way before with another woman. Somehow you and that sweet girl of yours have managed to get under his skin. And it's about time."

"Oh, Tilda, I never planned for anything to happen. But now that we're leaving, I won't be seeing Alex again."

She frowned. "I know Alex can be stubborn and difficult at times, but he hasn't had much love, or family, in his life. So if he backs away, or gets distant, don't give up on him. There's a pretty wonderful guy hidden inside."

Allison blinked at tears. "I have to put Cherry first."

"Of course you do, and he could help you with her. I believe that you care about him, too."

Care? She was close to falling in love with him. All Allison could do was nod.

"Good." With a smile, the older woman looked out of the window. "Land sake's, would you look at this?"

Allison turned around and saw two riders coming toward them. It was Alex on the gelding, leading Cherry on Maisie, and also Honey.

"I'd say the man's got it bad," Tilda said.

Allison ignored Tilda's comments as they walked outside. Alex climbed off his horse and one of the hands helped with the others.

"Hi, Mommy," Cherry called with a wave.

"Hi, sweetie." Her daughter had on jeans and a T-shirt. On her head she had a new cowboy hat. No doubt who it came from. "You're getting pretty good at riding Maisie."

"I know. Alex said we can all go riding. You, too."

Alex came across the porch with that lazy gait that caused her stomach to do a funny flip.

"I thought it would be nice if we all took a ride together."

That wasn't a good idea. "I can't leave everything for Tilda."

"It will be here when you get back." The older woman nudged her. "Now, go change. You can't keep them waiting."

Allison glanced at the happiness on Cherry's face. This was their last day here. How could she turn them down? "Okay, just give me a little time to change."

"Hurry, Mom, Alex's taking us to a secret place. And he says it's just for special girls."

* * *

Allison changed her clothes, came back outside and mounted Honey in record time. When she asked Alex where they were going, he refused to say, only instructed her and Cherry to follow him through the open pasture.

Allison watched her daughter, surprised how well she handled the pony. Although Alex had a lead rope, Cherry gave commands and handled the animal's reins. Allison glanced down at the child's jean-clad legs and saw a slight movement.

Allison's heart stopped and then began to race. She shot a look at Alex, who'd been watching her. He shook his head in warning, silently asking her not to say anything.

She rode up beside him. "Did you see what she did?"

Alex kept his gaze forward. "Yes, but I don't think she does. If we say something she might try too hard to do more than she can handle right now."

No matter what had happened between her and Alex, she knew he cared for Cherry. "You're right." She started to fall back behind her daughter, then stopped and touched his arm. "Thank you, Alex. Thank you for all you've done for my child."

He shrugged. "All I did was put her on a horse."

"And helped with her therapy, and took the time to teach her to ride. Oh, no, you didn't do much."

Alex watched Allison blink back tears and it nearly killed him. He regretted leaving her last night, but not as much as not being able to promise her a future.

"We'll never forget you," she whispered.

Unable to speak past the lump in his throat, he nodded, and she turned her horse around and fell back in behind her daughter. He would never be able to forget them either. Yet, the reality was she was leaving today.

Today. She and Cherry would be out of his life. It surprised him how much of his time had been filled with the two of them. How much he'd looked forward to seeing them every day.

He rode his horse through a grove of ancient oaks as they began to climb the gentle grade.

He turned back to Cherry. "Are you doing okay?"

The four-year-old nodded, concentrating hard on her task. Once again, Alex caught the slight movement of her tiny legs against the pony's flanks. He couldn't help but smile as the girl mimicked a clicking sound he'd made many times.

"We're almost there," he assured the riders. He finished the slight climb to the top of the hill. As soon as the ground leveled out, he stopped and looked at the incredible scenery. He moved the gelding into the sun for a better view of the ranch. Dense trees covered the slopes to the northwest, rich pasture land where his cattle grazed was to the east, and to the south ran one of the two creeks on the property that was lined with thick mesquite bushes. Cypress and cedars dotted the waterline.

"Oh, Alex," Allison gasped as she rode up beside him, her gaze roaming over the miles of his land. The bright hues of greens met the rich blue sky, mixing with the golden colors of the setting sun.

"Is this your secret place?" Cherry asked.

"In a way it is because I come here to see how pretty the world is. It always makes me feel better. But there is something else I want to share with you." He climbed down and came around to Cherry. After he unfastened her safety straps, he lifted her into his arms. He called to Allison over his shoulder. "Come on, Mom, you've got to see it, too."

They walked a ways back through the trees. It was almost forest-like when they came to a small clearing and a giant oak. The majestic tree reached high to the sky and its branches stretched out in all directions, shading the ground. The stocky trunk was covered with a rough bark and a hardy base with massive roots burrowing into the earth.

"It's a giant," Cherry called. "It's so big you can live in it."

"I don't know about that." Alex carried Cherry over and placed her on one of the low-hanging branches. "But it's big enough so a little girl can sit for awhile."

She giggled, balancing herself. "Wow! Mom, look at me."

"I see," Allison said, coming up next to him. "You be careful."

Alex couldn't resist. "Maybe you want to stay close by to make sure." He gripped Allison by her waist, and, ignoring her gasp, lifted her up next to her daughter.

"Alex!" she cried. "You can't lift me."

He grinned and stood back. "Looks like I already did." He reached into his pocket and pulled out his cell phone. "I think we need a picture of this day. So smile, ladies."

When both mother and daughter turned to him, smiling, he could barely concentrate on taking the photo. His chest tightened and he found he couldn't breathe, realizing how much they'd both come to mean to him. He didn't want to let them go, not yet.

Not ever.

CHAPTER NINE

IN A flash, her time at the A Bar A Ranch was a distant memory. No more rides to the creek, or to special places with amazing views. Most of all, no more rugged cowboy with steel-gray eyes and a touch that melted any resistance. Allison's heart fluttered as she recalled his kisses, his hands on her skin. His husky voice could send shivers down her spine. Then he turned on one of those rare smiles, or the gentle calming words that reassured her little girl her world seemed right.

It was past ten o'clock when Allison drove her loaded car back to Kerry Springs. She brushed away a wayward tear. Stop it, she chided. She'd known this was going to happen. Alex Casali wasn't the kind of man who would want to settle down with a woman and a kid. How many times had he said just that? He liked his life the way it was. No complications.

Fine. She didn't need him, either. All she needed was Cherry. All her attention had to be focused on her daughter to help get her well again. For the first time in a long time, she had hopes that would happen.

She drove through the alley at the back of her store and glanced in her mirror to catch the familiar truck headlights. Alex pulled up behind her. After getting out, she went to unlock the door while Alex took Cherry out of the car. Her daughter whimpered a little, but quieted with his soothing voice. He carried her inside and up to the apartment. Allison brought in two of their bags and made her way upstairs.

Alex met her halfway. "I'll get these. Go take care of Cherry."

She bit back any retort that might make him leave. "Thanks." She climbed the stairs and turned on the air conditioner, trying to cool off the small apartment before she went into her daughter's room.

"Mommy, it's too hot," the child complained. "I don't want to stay here."

"Honey, we've talked about this. This is our home." Allison bit back her own frustration, hating that she couldn't give her daughter something better.

Downstairs, Alex unloaded the boxes from the vehicles and stacked them in the storeroom on the first floor. He had to fight the urge to put everything back in the truck—including Allison and Cherry—and take them back to the ranch.

He rested his hands on his hips and looked around the cramped area. How could he leave them here? There wasn't enough room, and the apartment wasn't any better. He had to get them back to the ranch. He paused. And what? How would he keep them there? What could he offer her? To share his bed? No, Allison wouldn't go for it, and he couldn't blame her.

He carried the rest of the suitcases upstairs as Allison was coming out of the bedroom. "If you don't mind, would you say goodnight to Cherry?"

"Of course I will."

He put on a smile and walked into the bedroom. "Hey, little one. You're all tucked in."

She nodded. "But I don't like it here. I want to go back to the ranch."

He wanted the same thing. He sat down on the twin mattress. "It's not so bad. Your room is pretty." He could see that Allison had worked to decorate the small space. What made him angry was he could easily give both of them everything their hearts desired, including the best therapy room and treatment for Cherry.

Allison left Alex alone to say goodnight to her daughter. She could tell by his body language that he didn't want to stay. Well, she hadn't wanted to start anything in the beginning. He'd been the one who pursued her, the one who'd gotten involved in her life.

Made her care about him.

Alex came out of the bedroom. "She's asleep," he said as he walked toward where Allison stood in the kitchen area. "She's pretty exhausted from the ride today."

"Thank you for helping with all the boxes. Mostly for making our stay at the ranch so nice."

He shrugged. "It wasn't a big deal."

"No, I guess for you it wasn't. For my daughter, it was." Allison sighed. "I just have to figure out a way to get her to accept *normal* again."

He drew his eyebrows together in a frown. "I thought we decided that she would come to the ranch every week to ride."

"I don't know, Alex, if that's a good idea. Cherry will want more and more." She finally looked at him and wanted to shout, *It's you she wants. So do it.* She quickly glanced away. "I don't want her to be disappointed, or hurt."

He stood his ground. "And I don't want that girl to go without."

She closed her eyes a moment. "She isn't going without, Alex. I can give my daughter everything she needs."

"I know you can. I was just trying to take away some of your burden."

She fought her anger. "Cherry's not a burden."

"Dammit, that's not what I mean. But you have to work. You can't be everywhere." He reached for her. "I can afford to help you."

"In exchange for what, Alex? Are you suddenly changing your mind about taking me to your bed?"

He cursed. "I'm not asking for any strings, Allie," he said.

Hearing the endearment, she had to step back. She cared too much to let him do this. It would only be harder when he tired of her.

"Please Alex, you should go. I can't deal with this right now. Under the circumstances, us coming to the ranch is only going to complicate things more."

Alex stood his ground. He knew it was already too late, but he couldn't just walk away. "Maybe we should see where it leads."

She shook her head. "You don't want to do that, Alex. You like your life on your ranch away from everyone."

"That's not true. I have Tilda and Brian. Maybe I want to include you and Cherry in that group. I care about you both."

"And I care about you, too," she admitted. "Oh, Alex, I don't know if you can give us what we need. I'm not sure if we're what you want, either. I've already had a bad marriage. My record isn't very good."

He reached for her, bringing her close. "I didn't know we were keeping score. If so, add this in on the positive side." He leaned down and closed his mouth over hers, not wanting to give her a chance to back away from him again.

He drew back a fraction. "God, Allie, I want you. You want me, too. Nothing will ever change that."

She was breathless. "That's not the problem, Alex. But what if it doesn't go beyond that? For Cherry's sake, I can't risk it. I can't give her a taste of something so wonderful, and then take it away. She's already lost so much, including her father." She swallowed. "She's so attached to you. I can't have her lose you, too."

His chest ached. "What if I don't want to lose either of you?"

She smiled through watery eyes. "You haven't lost us, Alex. You just don't know where we fit in. You need to figure that out." She hesitated. "Maybe if you started by making peace with your past."

He hated that she made sense.

"You have a family, Alex," she went on. "It's far away in Italy, but they're extending a hand to you and your brother."

He tensed. "They haven't contacted either of us in years, and suddenly they want to include us?"

"There could have been a reason."

Alex crossed the room. He couldn't bring himself to tell her any more than he already had about his awful childhood. How abandoned he'd felt most of his life. God, he'd never do that to a child. He could never leave Cherry like that. He cared for the little one too much. He froze as he stared at Allison. He cared for her mother, too.

She came up to him. "I know this is hard for you, Alex. Good or bad, they're still your family."

He'd prayed for years someone would come for him and Angelo. To take them away from their mother, give them a home.

Allison touched his arm, making him look at her. "Do you have any idea how much I would love to have a relative out there? I was eight years old when I lost my parents. My grandmother took me in, but she died when I was in college. I only have Cherry." She blinked at threatening tears. "I nearly lost her. Now, you have the opportunity to talk things out with your father." She hesitated. "He isn't getting any younger. God forbid something happened and you'd let this chance slip by."

Alex swallowed back the dryness in his throat. Would his father even talk with him? Since he'd gotten Isabella's email and the wedding invitation, it had sparked curiosity about his family. It had also brought back feelings of hurt and despair that had been with him all his life.

"I don't know if I can do this, Allie," he admitted, his gaze meeting hers. "Not without help."

"I'll help in any way I can," she offered.

He leaned forward and brushed his mouth over hers. "If you mean that, then come to Italy with me."

Five days later, Allison was calling herself crazy as she buckled her seat belt on Alex's private plane. The sleek Learjet's interior was decorated in shades of gray and burgundy with comfortable captain's chairs and even a sleeping area for long flights.

Looking across to the window seat, she saw her daughter's smiling face and stopped berating herself. They were going to Italy. Thank goodness they'd had passports from a previous trip to Canada to see a doctor.

After finding someone to watch Blind Stitch, and rescheduling Cherry's therapy, she felt a little giddy just thinking about the trip.

In the front of the cabin, Alex was talking with the pilot. He'd left his hat and western clothes back at the ranch, replaced by a pair of charcoal dress trousers and a white oxford cloth shirt opened at the neck. Yet, he wore a pair of shiny black cowboy boots.

Once Alex ended the instructions, he pulled out his cell phone. During the call, he frowned as he nodded, then by the end of the talk his expression turned sad. She knew he'd been trying to convince Angelo to go with them. It looked as if he wasn't making any headway. He shut his phone and said something to the pilot, then he sat down in the seat next to hers.

He touched Cherry's arm. "You ready to go flying, *uccellino*?"

She nodded enthusiastically. "I want to go up to the clouds."

"Then we're in luck. That's where Captain Jason is taking us." He turned to Allison. "Are you all right?"

She nodded, too. "What's not to be all right about? I'm flying to Europe, and on a private jet."

"I'm glad you're enjoying it."

She sobered. "You're the one I'm worried about. I'm afraid I rushed you into this trip."

"I don't have the luxury of waiting. Roundup is coming in another month. I have beef orders to fill. So it's as good a time as any to get this over with."

He didn't sound happy. "Poor you, you've got to go to ugly old Italy."

He tried to glare at her, but it didn't work.

"It's all right, Alex," she began. "I'm sure Brian can

handle things. And Tilda has finally got you out from underfoot."

His glare intensified. "Did she say that?"

She sighed. "Look, Tilda loves you like a son. She only wants you to be happy. We're both hoping this will help you. So tell me about this family of yours. Are you related to royalty, or anyone famous?"

He gave her an annoyed look.

"Come on, Alex. You can't tell me you haven't investigated your roots." All she'd gotten from him was he was born and lived three years of his life in a small town called Monta Correnti between Rome and Naples.

He shook his head. "I know only what my mother told me." He looked at her. "When she'd been sober enough to talk about it."

Allison watched the emotions play across his face, knowing none of this was easy for him.

He began the story. "Seems the interesting part began with my paternal grandmother, Rosa Casali. She was sixteen when her family arranged her marriage to an older man, Roberto Firenzi, and they had two children, Lisa and Luigi.

"During the Second World War Rosa volunteered at a hospital where she cared for a wounded English soldier, William Valentine. After three weeks, they couldn't resist temptation any longer and spent the night together."

Hearing the jet engines, Allison checked on Cherry, but quickly turned to Alex, wanting to hear more. "Did William ever come back for her? Was he killed?"

Alex shook his head. "No, but it seems before he left he gave her a secret recipe for tomato sauce. That last day after she said goodbye to William, her husband

Roberto died. Just weeks later, Rosa also discovered she was pregnant with my father, Luca."

How wonderful that Rosa found love, Allison thought. "What did she do?"

"Having to support her family, Rosa sold everything she could and opened the restaurant, Sorella. My father worked there along with his sister, Lisa, but they never got along. And it got worse and after Rosa died, Luca struck out on his own. He started up a roadside food stand. That was when our mother, Cindy Daniels, came through the village on vacation from the states. Their attraction was instant and they quickly married. Soon after, my brother and I arrived."

"I bet you two were a handful," Allison said.

"According to our mother, Luca didn't help at all, he ignored her. So she divorced him, and left us all and returned home to Boston. A year or so later, Luca shipped us off to her. End of story."

Allison doubted it was the end, but she could see Alex wasn't about to say any more. "I guess you'll have to hear your father's side of the story."

Alex shrugged and scooted down in his seat. "You're hoping for a miracle."

She reached for his hand. "It'll be okay, Alex." She sent up a prayer hoping that was true as the plane headed off down the runway. She glanced at the man who'd stolen her heart.

There was no going back now, for either of them.

Sometime later that evening the plane landed in Naples. Allison was surprised that Cherry had slept on and off during the long flight. They'd played games and watched videos, even did some leg exercises, and then she finally drifted off to sleep. Allison hadn't been so lucky. Sleep eluded her, and Alex stayed busy with work he'd brought along.

Once they got off the plane and through customs, there was a car waiting for them. The darkness made it impossible to see any scenery and Allison was too tired to care. After the car was loaded with their luggage and portable wheelchair purchased for the trip, they took off to where they were going to stay.

About thirty minutes later they pulled up in front of a large villa. Even in the dark she could see the building's grandeur. Suddenly the car door opened and Alex stepped out. She heard a greeting exchanged in Italian, then he leaned in and reached for Cherry. "I'll get her."

He adjusted the child in his arms as Allison climbed out. She tried to brush the wrinkles from her clothes, but gave up.

"*Signora*, welcome to Villa Monte Vista. I hope you enjoy your stay with us. My name is Stefano and my wife is Ghita. She is preparing you a light meal."

"Thank you."

The man in his fifties bowed and motioned to the young boy to come toward the car. "And this is our son, Tomasso." The teenager nodded. "Allow me to show you to your rooms," Stefano said as his son began to load the luggage on the cart as they walked up the path.

They continued on through the tall carved doors and into an enormous entry with marble floors and rough, golden-hued walls. A huge staircase angled against one wall; the steps were partly covered by a beautiful carpet runner.

They took an elevator just under the stairs. After it reached the second floor, they stepped out into a sitting area where there was a table with a large bouquet of fresh flowers. The heavenly fragrance followed them down a wide hall until they came to a set of double doors. Stefano pushed them open and stood aside, allowing them to enter a sitting area with overstuffed sofas and a large tiled fireplace. He then took them to a room with a huge bed decorated with a rich wine-colored satin comforter. She couldn't help but wonder if Alex had planned to stay in here with her.

Stefano instructed his son to leave Allison's luggage, then he walked over to an alcove where there was a single bed. The bright yellow coverings were pulled back, revealing snowy white sheets.

He smiled. "This is for the *bambina*."

"It's perfect," Allison said. "Thank you."

Alex placed the sleeping Cherry on the mattress and Allison went to remove her shoes and took off her jeans. The child didn't even stir. In the end, Allison left her in her T-shirt and underwear for this once. With a kiss on her daughter's forehead, she turned on the night-light and went back to the sitting room.

Allison followed the voices into another doorway across from hers. This room was smaller with a cream and gold décor. She glanced at the queen-sized bed.

Alex turned to her as Tomasso brought in his luggage. "Is your room close enough to Cherry?"

She nodded. "It's perfect." She turned to Stefano. "Thank you."

He bowed again. "You're very welcome, *signora*." Another few minutes, they finished their task and left.

"Alex, you didn't need to give up your room," Allison said. "Cherry and I can easily fit in this bed together."

"I want you to be comfortable."

"What about you? This bed can't be big enough for you."

"I'll survive."

She caught his heated gaze and quickly glanced away.

"There's food in the sitting area," he said. "Some cheese, bread and wine. Join me."

That wouldn't be wise. "I think I'll shower first."

He nodded. "Good idea." Then he left for his room.

She had seen the stress etched on his face, and nearly called him back, but she was better off to keep a safe distance.

After hearing the door close, she went to get her pajamas and robe out of her bag. In the spacious private bathroom, she turned on the shower and let the water relieve the tension of her long day.

Fifteen minutes later she felt much better. She checked on Cherry, then peered into the other room, and found Alex outside the French door standing on the balcony.

She started to leave when he called to her.

"Are you afraid to be alone with me?"

She looked back to see he had on the same trousers, but a fresh black T-shirt. It outlined the muscles in his chest and arms.

She pulled together her cotton robe and came forward. "I just didn't want to disturb you. You have a lot on your mind. Does your family know you arrived?"

"Only my sister, Isabella." He shook his head. "Man, that's crazy. Suddenly I have a sister and two more brothers. How am I supposed to act with them?"

"Don't act." She felt her mouth fighting a smile. "Just be yourself."

He threw his head back and laughed. "That should go over well."

"What I mean is be your *charming* self."

Alex's gaze connected with hers. He tried not to notice how good she looked, how her red hair brushed against her shoulders, recalling how it felt like to touch. Even dressed in simple satin pajama bottoms and tank top didn't take away from her sex appeal. He could see her nervousness as she tugged on her robe to cover her enticing body.

He didn't think it was possible to miss someone so much in just a few minutes. He crossed the room and took her hand. "Come, have a glass of wine."

"I should go to bed." She resisted, but let him lead her to the table where he poured her a glass.

"You can't come all the way to Italy and not sample the local vintage." He handed her a goblet. "Stefano informed me it's from a winery not far from here."

She held her glass up, then took a hesitant sip. "Oh, it is wonderful." She nodded. "You should taste it."

Mesmerized, he watched her press her lips against the crystal goblet. He put his glass down and came to her. "I'd rather taste you." He dipped his head and caught her mouth as she gasped. Next came a soft moan and she melted against him. She felt good. She tasted good. Who needed wine?

The next morning, Allison awoke early and immediately her thoughts turned to Alex. She wasn't happy that she had nearly given into her feelings for him. The man knew how to push the right buttons. Of course, she half expected that he would take advantage of the situation. And being in romantic Italy had nothing to do with her wanting the man.

She knew he'd be a tender and considerate lover, but

she needed more than the physical side. When the trip was over where did they go from here? She was definitely in love with the Texas rancher. Late last night, they'd both been willing, but in the end they'd parted and gone off to their separate rooms.

Thirty minutes later, both she and Cherry were dressed and ready for breakfast. With Stefano's help, Allison took Cherry down to the patio. Seeing her daughter's excitement, she knew that this trip was worth it.

Allison went to the wrought-iron railing, excited as she scanned the beautiful scenery surrounding her. Lush green foliage covered miles of rolling hills. Off in the distance she could see groups of salmon-hued structures in the neighboring village. Was this Monta Correnti? Was it where Alex's family lived? Where he had been born?

A warm breeze caught her hair and she closed her eyes, praying that everything worked out for him.

"Mommy?"

She turned around. "What, sweetie?"

Her daughter was dressed in a pair of black tights and a red and white jumper-style dress. Her blonde curls were pulled back into a ponytail. "Does Alex's family have any little kids?"

Allison still got a rush when she heard Cherry speak. "I'm not sure. You'll have to ask Alex."

"Ask me what, little one?" He came through the door and leaned down and kissed Cherry on the cheek. She looked up at him with adoring eyes. She wasn't immune to the man, either.

"Do you have any little girls in your family?"

"I'm not sure. But we'll find out soon."

He walked to Allison and kissed her full on the

mouth. "Good morning," he whispered. "Just so you know, I had a restless night." His gaze met hers. "I kept dreaming of you."

Allison felt a blush creeping up her face as she glanced at Cherry's smile. "I slept very well."

With his grin, her heart raced. "You're not a very good liar, Allie Cole."

She kept watching him. Those steel-gray eyes locked on hers, and she couldn't manage any words. Afraid was more like it, that she might confess her feelings. And he wasn't ready for her. He might never be. "You don't need any distractions right now."

Stefano appeared in the doorway. "Excuse me, *signore* and *signora*. But you have a guest."

Before Stefano could announce her, a young woman came rushing out. She had long black hair, olive skin and stood a little taller than Allison and she had a curvaceous body to die for. She smiled brightly as she looked directly at Alex. She quickly closed the distance between them and kissed both his cheeks.

"Oh, Alessandro, I'd know you anywhere. Welcome home, *fratello*, brother."

CHAPTER TEN

ALEX hadn't been sure what to expect on coming to Italy. Now, seeing this beautiful woman, his sister, created feelings in him he couldn't express in mere words.

He glanced toward the patio doors, wishing Allison would change her mind and return to help get him through this. After a short exchange of pleasantries, Allison had excused herself and taken Cherry and left.

He turned back to Isabella. Even after learning everything he could about his childhood here, Alex was still thrown off seeing a family member.

And she was his sister. God, he wished he had known about her. Maybe things would have been different. But he'd been excluded.

"I can't tell you how happy I am that you decided to come home," Isabella told him.

He tensed. "This isn't my home. Angelo and I were sent away. It's hard to consider this my home. It's hard getting used to you being my family."

Dark blue eyes stared back at him, not wavering. Nearly black hair hung loose, her skin rich olive.

"Over the years many mistakes and misunderstandings have occurred," Isabella began. "Our father would have never sent you to America if he knew what kind of life you lived there. He tried to stay in touch, but your mother moved so often, our papa lost track of you, Alessandro."

Alex tensed on hearing his given name. "Seems to be a good excuse, but, to me and my brother, he just didn't try very hard to find us. By the way, my name is Alex." He'd made the change years ago when kids had made fun of his name. And when he'd been old enough to discover that he'd been abandoned by the father who'd chosen it.

She smiled easily. "I can see you are as stubborn as he is." She waved her hand in the air. "Please, this is not the time to argue about this. One of my *grandi fratelli* has come home from America."

"*Fratellastro*. I'm your half-brother."

Tears filled her eyes. "You're still of my blood, Alex. *Famigila.* Family. And everyone wants to get to know you as much as I do."

He stiffened. "I asked you not to tell anyone. I refuse to be scrutinized on my reasons for coming here."

"And I honored your wishes. It's just from the moment the secret came out about yours and Angelo's existence, we've all been eager to meet you." She arched an eyebrow. "We would also like to know Allison and Cherry. It's easy to see how much they mean to you."

Alex wasn't going to give into Isabella's speculation. It was none of their business. "She worked at my guest ranch, and I help her with her daughter."

"Oh, men. It is so difficult to admit your feelings? They are both *bellissima.*"

He glared at her, then gave a nod of agreement.

She laughed and the sweet sound tugged at him. "I can't wait for you to meet my husband, Max. Then you'll understand why you don't intimidate me." She gave another bright smile. "Please, you didn't come all this way not to give us a chance to be a family." She pulled out a card. "Come to the family restaurant. Rosa."

Alex took the card. This was the hard part, finally facing his past. "When?"

Isabella released a sigh. "Tonight. If that's convenient, of course."

He'd waited years for this. Years to face his father. Maybe he'd finally get the answers he needed so he could move on. "We'll be there."

"That's all I can ask." She smiled as they walked toward the doors at the front of the villa. She rose up and kissed both his cheeks. "Please tell Allison I look forward to seeing her tonight. *Ciao.*" She waved and got into her car and drove off.

Alex returned to the patio. He stood at the wrought-iron railing that overlooked the beautiful countryside. He and Angelo had been born here.

"Alex?"

He turned around as Allison walked toward him. He managed to smile.

"Isabella is lovely. But I know it had to be rough on you to see her."

"You mean all the years I missed watching her grow up?"

She nodded. "You're here now. You can share her life now."

He pulled her close, even though he didn't want to need her. "Sometimes I wonder if I'll ever belong anywhere."

"Then let's find out. You can't stay cooped up all day when there's all this beautiful country to see."

He opened his mouth to disagree.

"Don't say you'd rather be inside today. Not a man who rides the borders of his vast land."

He frowned. "How did you know?"

She smiled. "I didn't, but you're not the type of man who likes being inside for long."

"You think you know me so well?"

"I don't think you let anyone that close." She put on a smile again. "Come on, let's take Cherry into the village." She tugged on his arm. "We'll pretend we're tourists."

He found he enjoyed playing her game. "We are."

"I said we're pretending."

That he could do, since he'd been pretending all his life.

Later that evening, Allison sat with Cherry in the backseat of the town car as they headed to Monta Correnti. She glanced toward the front passenger seat to where Alex rode. They'd had fun today. They'd taken Cherry around the grounds, then into the small village where they'd bought silly souvenir trinkets.

By the time they got home and put Cherry down for a nap, Alex had pulled inside himself once again. She knew he'd started thinking about seeing his family.

She hoped that once he met with them he could find some peace. Seeing the tension on his face, she couldn't help but wonder if she'd been wrong to suggest he come to Italy.

Allison glanced out of the window at the exquisite scenery. Earlier today, Stefano had told them about Alex's birthplace, the rolling hillsides with small farms and villages that dotted the landscape. The car drove down a hill and Lake Adrina came into view. The water was a crystal-clear blue, reflecting the sun setting behind the hills.

A while later, the car slowed as they came to the edge of town. There were narrow streets and rows of stairways ran in between a maze of ancient buildings. The quaint hillside structures reminded her of an artist's painting.

Her heart began to race as she wondered how Alex was handling all this. Did he remember any of it? She wanted to reach for him, help him through it.

In the front seat Alex tried not to react as they drove into Monta Correnti. The narrow streets took him back in time, but only served to heighten his interest in learning more about his past. They came to the town square, but nothing there triggered a memory. Finally the car stopped in front of a stucco-coated building with a wrought-iron-trimmed courtyard. A sign overhead read, "Rosa Ristorante".

Alex ignored the pulse pounding in his ears. He climbed out and glanced at the people dining outside, then turned to open the back door. He peered in and met Allison's gaze.

She looked concerned. "Are you sure you want us here?"

He wanted to pull her out of the car and into his arms, but he'd always done things on his own. Besides Angelo, he wasn't sure he was capable of trusting anyone. Every time he had, he'd been the one who lost. "I'm not sure I want to be here."

She placed a hand on his arm. "Then I'm glad we're with you."

"Alex, do I get to see your papa?" Cherry asked.

Alex wasn't sure. Of anything. Isabella had been the only one he'd contacted about his visit. "He's supposed to be here. This is his restaurant." He released a breath. "So let's go see."

He helped Allison out and gave her a long look. She had on a burgundy-colored sundress that flattered her trim body. Her hair was pulled back away from her pretty face and large sterling hoops hung from her ears.

"Am I dressed all right?"

"You're perfect."

He reached in the car and lifted Cherry out. He placed her in her chair that Stefano had waiting. "And you look pretty as a princess." Her sundress was blue and her hair was pulled back in a ponytail.

As they turned around Isabella came rushing out of the entrance dressed in a white chef's uniform. "Oh, you came." She reached up and kissed his cheeks, then Allison and Cherry.

"Oh, *uccellino*."

Cherry giggled. "Alex calls me that name."

Alex's gaze shot to Allison, then to Isabella. His sister didn't miss his surprise. "And that's what our papa called me from the time I was a *bambina*."

Alex didn't want to think he'd remembered all those years ago, but the fact was he must have. Had his father used the same endearment towards him and his brother Angelo?

"Come, let us go inside," Isabella said.

Alex resisted. "Is everyone here?"

Isabella shook her head. "Heavens, no. Luca is here, of course. It's impossible to get him to stay away from this place. I also work here. Please, Alessandro, it will be okay." She gave him a sassy wink. "I will protect you if anyone treats you bad."

Alex couldn't help but smile. She probably would. He glanced at Allison. He'd already experienced the woman's strength. "I guess I have enough protection."

After walking through the courtyard filled with guests, Stefano held open the door to allow them to enter the dimly lit entryway. Alex glanced around the restaurant that had been named after his grandmother Rosa. The rustic setting had frescoed walls and terracotta floors and was sectioned off into different areas. Rosa's served traditional, home-cooked Italian food, and, by the size of the vociferous crowd, it was successful. Many of the tables were filled with people and the sounds of laughter and shouts were almost overwhelming.

Isabella stopped by one of the white-clothed tables and spoke with some guests. She then motioned for Alex to follow her. He started to push Cherry's wheelchair, but Allison stopped him.

"Alex, why don't I let you talk to your father first?" She smiled. "Cherry and I need to make a trip to the rest room, so we'll be back in a few minutes."

He wasn't convinced he wanted to do this either.

"You've waited a long time for this day. This is between you and your father. We'll be back in a little while." She nodded. "Now, go."

She gave him an encouraging smile. He started to disagree, but he could only watch as she and Cherry started off toward the lounge.

Isabella called over one of the restaurant's hostesses and spoke to her. The young girl followed after Allison. "They'll be looked after," she said as she took his arm and led him toward the back of the restaurant and into an alcove. A semi-private area in the back of the restaurant was set aside for larger parties.

He looked around, trying to picture his father. Even with a photo, he wasn't sure if he would recognize him. Would Luca know him?

Suddenly he heard voices as the kitchen door swung open. An older man walked out. His head was turned away, calling to someone over his shoulder, then he spoke to a few guests before finally looking in their direction. He saw Isabella and smiled and his steps got more determined.

Alex's heart lodged in his throat. The man he'd once called Papa was tall with a slender build. His gray-streaked hair was cut short, his narrow face showed many years of life. It seemed that Luca Casali had lived his sixty-seven years to the fullest.

Slowly Luca's gaze locked on him. His smile faded as his steps faltered. A look of panic crossed his face, then it seemed to change to sadness. At that moment, Alex once again felt like the unwanted child that had been sent away.

"Papa…" Isabella began, but she was ignored as he continued toward Alex.

Luca stopped in front of him. "Alessandro," he whispered as tears welled up his clear blue eyes. "Oh, God, Alessandro."

All Alex could do was nod, trying to ignore his own emotions, but it was hard. "I go by Alex now."

Luca seemed to freeze, not knowing what to do next. It was Isabella who stepped in. "Papa, Alex came all the way from America to see us." The noise level seemed to rise. "Come, let's move some place a little more private."

She led the two men into the alcove, then closed the louvered folding doors, muffling the outside noise. She motioned to a long table covered in linen. "Sit," she instructed the two men. "I'll get the wine." Before they could stop her, Isabella had slipped out once again.

Alex didn't speak. He couldn't if he wanted to.

Besides, he'd come all this way to hear this man's explanation. What he hated the most was that he wanted Luca Casali to have a good reason why he'd sent them away.

Luca took a long time to speak. "I've prayed for this day."

"I stopped praying a long time ago."

Tears filled the older man's eyes again as he stood there and took what Alex was handing out. "I don't blame you and your brother for hating me."

Alex felt his control slipping. "Believe me, I've had years to perfect it."

"I'm sorry, *figlio*. So sorry. There is no excuse for what I did."

Alex straightened. "How can you call me your son? For years you denied us."

Just then Isabella came through the door carrying a bottle with glasses with Allison and Cherry following her.

"Look who's joining us." His sister smiled. "Papa, this is Alex's friend, Allison Cole and her daughter, Cherry."

Luca went to Allison and took her hand. "I'm pleased to meet you," he said, then looked down at Cherry. "Aren't you a *bella signorina*? Just like your mother."

Cherry blushed. "Thank you. Are you Alex's papa?" she asked boldly.

Luca looked sad. "I'm sorry to say not for a very long time."

Alex tensed and Isabella saw it. "Please, Alex. Papa. Everyone, let's sit down and have a drink together. We'll talk."

Alex wasn't sure if he could; his feelings were too close to the surface. "What should we drink to? The long-lost son returns?"

His sister handed Alex a glass and Allison one, too.

132 THE COWBOY'S ADOPTED DAUGHTER

"Yes, for one. And to hear Papa's side of what happened all those years ago." She turned to Luca. "Papa, tell him why you had to let them go. Why you didn't have any other choice."

Luca looked at his daughter. "It doesn't matter the reason. I did the unforgivable and sent my *figlios* away." He took a long drink from his glass. "I thought you needed to be with your mother."

Alex drained his glass. "You wanted to be rid of us."

"Never," Luca denied, his gaze not wavering from his son. "I couldn't afford to keep you with me. Business was bad then, and I had to work all the time. There was no money, no one to watch you and Angelo. I thought sending you to your mother would be best."

He saw Allison get up and take Cherry out of the room. He wanted to go after her, but things needed to be said. "Well, you thought wrong," Alex threw back, but kept his voice low and controlled. "Cindy didn't take care of us. She was a drunk. We went hungry, several times we were out on the streets. And when she was home, all she did was moan about you. She wanted you to come to her."

Luca looked wounded by the words and Alex wished he'd gotten satisfaction, but he hadn't. But it didn't stop him. "Cindy didn't want Angelo or me, and neither did you. You were a great pair. It's surprising you didn't stay together."

The door opened and a man came in. He was shorter than Alex, but no less muscular. He had dark eyes and hair. He sent a glare toward Alex before he walked to Luca and placed a hand on his shoulder. "Papa, is there a problem?"

Luca shook his head. "Of course not. Valentino, I'd

like you to meet your older brother, Alessandro. Sorry, it's Alex. Alex, this is your brother, Valentino."

Alex nodded. Earlier today Isabella had told him more about his half-siblings, Cristiano, a firefighter who lived in Rome, and Valentino the race-car driver who lived in town. His sister had tossed out another zinger earlier when she had also told him that Valentino wasn't actually Alex's biological brother. Apparently Luca's second wife, Violetta, had had an affair during their marriage. Luca had raised Valentino as his own child.

Yet, Luca hadn't seemed able to keep in touch with his own twin sons. With hurt and anger building, Alex turned to his sister. "I can't deal with this right now."

Isabella looked panicked. "Of course, this is difficult for you." She touched his arm. "Please, let's make it another time."

Alex wasn't sure he could go through this again. Ever. He walked out of the room, glad no one followed him. He hated the feelings that churned inside him. He couldn't let anyone see them. Then he would lose all defenses.

Maybe Angelo had been smart to stay away. Maybe he shouldn't have come here, either. How could it help to drudge up old news, old memories? He'd still had a miserable childhood, and nothing would ever change that.

He was still on the outside looking in.

Alex had managed to get Allison and Cherry back into the car, but not without Isabella coming out to assist them. She'd packed up food to take with them back to the villa.

Cherry was soon distracted by having a picnic in the car. So during their impromptu meal of chicken and warm bread, Alex tried to explain to the child about his father.

By the time the thirty-minute drive ended as Stefano

pulled the car up in front of the villa, Cherry was sound asleep. Alex carried her upstairs without too many questions. Since he'd gotten the precious child to talk, that was all she did these days.

She was one of the highlights in all this. He realized that he wasn't anything like his father; he could never abandon a child. No matter what. Cherry had come to mean too much to him. If he was honest, so had Allison.

Alex came out into the main room. After pouring a glass of wine, he walked out onto the second-story balcony. A soft breeze cooled his face as he recalled the scene at the restaurant. All the years of anger, the abandonment, came rushing back. A father that had turned his back on him and his brother. He didn't want to rehash the reasons, more likely the excuses, that they all were handing out.

He took a swallow of wine, trying to dull the pain, but it was doing nothing. Why had he even answered Isabella's message? Why had he let her talk him into coming here? All that came from this trip was that he realized he didn't belong.

Well, he didn't need to be told again. As soon as he could make the arrangements, he would head back to the life he'd made for himself in Texas and forget about anyone connected with Monta Correnti.

Alex heard the door open from the master suite. He turned and saw Allison standing in the doorway. She was still wearing the same dress as earlier, but she'd taken her hair down, the way he liked it. But then, he wanted Allison any way he could have her.

He drank the last of his wine and set his glass on the table. He crossed the patio, pulled her into his arms and kissed her. It was quick and hard, sparking his mood and need. He wasn't subtle about relaying what she did to him. He broke off the kiss. "I want you, Allie."

She placed her hands against his chest and pushed him back. "Oh, my, what every woman loves to hear. Besides, sex isn't going to take away the pain you're feeling."

"Hell, you could make me forget my name." He arched an eyebrow at her. "There's never been a doubt that I've wanted you. Even from the first day you came to the ranch. Why do you think I tried to drive you away?"

Allison was flattered and thrilled over the back-handed compliment. She was crazy about the man, but she couldn't help him do this. "That's just it, Alex. You want to drive everyone away. You can't take the chance of being rejected. Again."

He cursed. "I don't need to be analyzed by an amateur."

She couldn't back down. "Too bad about that. You wanted me to come here with you, so I get my say." She took a calming breath. "I came to support you through this time with your family. I know it's been difficult, but you aren't giving it a chance."

"There wasn't much to say. Luca shipped us to America to our mother. He had no regrets. No remorse. He said he couldn't keep us. There was no room in his life. End of story."

"Alex, there has to be more. I heard him apologize for misjudging the situation with his ex-wife."

He shrugged. "Okay, he said he didn't realize how bad things were. I might be able to understand that, but not even checking on us until we were eighteen?" He glared at her. "I thought I could handle the fact he kept us a secret from the rest of the family, that he denied our existence. But after tonight…"

It killed Allison to see his pain. "What?"

He poured another glass of wine and one for her. "It's not important."

She refused the drink. "It's important to you."

He took a long drink, then refilled the glass and paced across the tiled floor. "It seems funny to me that my father gave away his own sons, but accepted a child who wasn't even his. His second wife had an affair and he took her back...pregnant." He turned to her. "He came in after you left—Valentino Casali. He actually looked at me as if I was the outsider. Like I didn't have a right to be here. He called Luca 'Papa'." Alex nearly choked on the words. "The guy acted as if I were the threat to my own father."

"I'm sorry, Alex. I'm truly sorry."

He glared at her. "Damn it. I don't want pity. I've had pity all my life." He walked to the railing. "I'm not a scared, lonely child any more. I've handled everything that's been dealt me. I have a successful life and money. I don't need to get approval from a family that never wanted me."

Allison saw his agony and she couldn't do anything for the man she loved. "Alex, don't push this aside as if it doesn't matter." She walked to him, wanting to comfort him. "He's your father."

"No! Luca was never my father and never will be. I don't need anyone."

"Everyone needs someone."

"I guess you just met the first, then." He grabbed the wine bottle off the table and stormed through the main room and into his bedroom, slamming the door behind him. The sound was deafening, but the silence afterward was worse. It felt so final.

Once again, Alex Casali had shut her out of his life.

CHAPTER ELEVEN

THE next morning, sunlight poured through the window and across the bed as Alex rolled over with a groan, then jerked upright. He glanced around the room, quickly remembering where he was. The clock on the bedside table read 9:00a.m.

With a curse, he stood, his stomach rolled, and pain seared through his head. He was still dressed in the same clothes as the day before. His muddled brain managed to recall incidents from the night before he'd rather forget. The trip into Monta Correnti. His father. The argument. Then back at the villa, he had taken out his anger on Allison. He groaned again, recalling things he'd said to her.

He headed for the bathroom. After a quick shower, he pulled on a pair of jeans and a shirt, and went in search of the woman who hadn't deserved his wrath. Allison. He hoped mother and daughter weren't up yet so he could clear his head with some coffee before he apologized for his rude behavior. Then he'd offer to take them sightseeing before heading back to Texas.

He knocked on their bedroom door. When there was no answer, he looked inside to find it empty. He hurried downstairs to the patio, expecting to find them eating breakfast. The place was deserted, too. He was about to pick up the house phone when Tomasso appeared.

"Have you seen the *signora* and the *bambina*?"

"*Sì.* They left with *mio papa*."

"Did they go into the village?"

The boy looked confused, then shook his head. "*Aeroporto.*"

His gut tightened. Allison had left him? "The airport. When? How long ago?"

The teenager spoke in rapid Italian. Alex wasn't in the mood to try to decipher the words. "I need an automobile."

The boy shook his head. "No automobile."

Alex cursed and took out his cell phone and punched the number for directory assistance. He walked into the house, where he spotted Luca Casali waiting in the entry.

Alex straightened. "What do you want?"

The older man was dressed in khaki trousers and an open-collar navy shirt. "I came to talk to my son," he said as he walked toward him. "Something I regret not doing years ago."

Alex didn't want this now. "You're right, but it's too late. Besides, I have something more important to do at the moment." He headed for the stairs.

"You're correct, Allison and Cherry are definitely worth your time."

He paused and turned around. "You know where they are?"

Luca nodded. "They're at the restaurant with Isabella and your cousin Lizzie." He smiled. "They are entertaining the lovely *bambina*." His expression grew serious. "It's a tragedy about her accident. I hear you've been instrumental in her recovery."

He eyed his father. "I might have helped some, but

until Cherry is walking again, it's not a full recovery. Now, if you'll excuse me, I have to go get them."

Luca raised a hand. "You have my word that they will not leave Monta Correnti until we've finished our discussion."

Alex was somewhat relieved. He'd have a chance to try and talk with Allison. Once they returned home to Texas he could straighten things out with her. He looked at Luca. He wasn't sure about his father. "We'll all be leaving today."

Luca only watched him a moment, then said, "You came all this way to meet family, Alessandro. Suddenly you changed your mind?"

He nodded. "I decided some things are better left alone. So give the family my regards, I'll be returning home."

The man didn't move. "*Per favore*, Alessandro. Don't cheat your brothers and sister out of their chance to get to know you because of how you feel about me."

"I don't fit in here," he blurted out.

"You are a Casali, of course you belong here. So don't let your anger at me keep you from your family." He spread his arms. "Maybe you can tell me what you've wanted to say for all the years that I wasn't there for you or for your brother. Now is your chance."

Alex's chest tightened as he felt an unwelcome pull to the man he didn't want or need. For all those years he'd had a hundred things he wanted to tell his absent father, but none of it seemed to matter now. Just Allison. "It's not important."

"It was important enough to bring you to Italy." His blue eyes searched Alex's face. "It's too many years past due that we meet again. For a father who hasn't seen his son since he was a boy."

"Whose fault is that?"

"*Sì*, it's mine. But it's also time that you know everything." He came closer. "I can…" Luca swallowed. "I can never ask or expect your forgiveness. Just know that when I sent you off to America, it wasn't because I didn't care, or love you and your brother. I couldn't afford to keep you, things were desperate here."

With a mother like Cindy, things had been desperate for Alex and Angelo, too. "I don't think you want to compare stories on who had the tougher life. But go for it."

His father shook his head. "Believe me, I had no idea how bad your situation became until years later. I admit I lost touch, but I had no idea what Cindy had done to you. What a horrid childhood for you and Angelo."

"Then you should have come to the States to find your sons." Alex glared at the man. "You owed us that. Instead you went and got another family. You claimed a child that wasn't yours." He folded his arms across his chest. "Well, damn, aren't you the noble one."

Sadness appeared in Luca's eyes. "It was because I had turned my back on my own sons that I needed to be there for Valentino. I wish I could have done more for you and Angelo, but I'd missed any chance of that." He paused. "And the things I've done, the mistakes I made over those years, will follow me to my grave."

"Is that how you've lived with yourself all these years?" Alex asked. "You put us so far out of your mind that we no longer existed to you?"

Luca ignored his words. "I wish I could take all the pain away. I can't, Alex. When I found you and Angelo again at eighteen, I called, but I let you push me out of your life too easily. I should have come for you then. I should have fought for my sons. I'm sorry, Alex. I'm so sorry for all those awful years that you and Angelo didn't have anyone to care for you, to protect you."

Alex felt the ache in the middle of his chest. He hated that the feelings he'd buried years ago had resurfaced. "Nice speech, but don't expect me to disagree, or to forgive you."

Luca shook his head. "That's not what I came here for."

"Then for what?"

"For you. You say none of this bothers you, yet I see the pain in your eyes, hear it in your voice. You have so much anger in your heart."

"Of course I have anger. You kept us a secret from the family. Were you that ashamed of us?"

A flash of hurt crossed the older man's face. "Not of you. Just the opposite. Of me. I was so ashamed that I couldn't keep you, that I couldn't be the father you needed. I'm very proud of what you and Angelo have become."

"Don't take any pride in us, because you had nothing to do with it."

"I think I did. I believe your anger for me helped drive you towards success. That's the only part I played in it. If you would like, I will sit down with you and admit to everything I did wrong, with your mother and with you and your brother. But when we finish, you need to let it go, Alex. To get rid of the anger before it kills your soul. Before you lose everything."

Alex hated the fact that this visit affected him so strongly. "I'm not losing anything."

"You're wrong, Alex. You're already driving away a family you have a chance to know. And what about Allison? You've driving her away, too."

"Leave her out of this."

Luca shook his head. "I can't. Not when she's so important to you. She's part of this, too. Yet you won't let her get close to you."

"And I'm supposed to take advice from you?" He saw the flash of hurt and regretted his harsh words. "Maybe you should leave now."

His father held his gaze. "I'm not going anywhere. At least not until we talk through this. You may not want to hear them, but I need to say them. We may never be father and son again, but I'll settle for being civil to one another."

Alex arched an eyebrow. "Isn't that aiming a little high for us?"

"Then do it for Allison. It's what she wants."

Alex didn't want to talk about Allison. "How do you know what she wants?"

Luca smiled. "She told me. The little one, too." His father's eyes locked on his. "It's such a shame, since you have the same opportunity to be a father to little Cherry. They both need you." Luca's face held sadness. "More importantly, you need them."

An hour later at Rosa's *ristorante* there was a collective gasp when the most recent family bride, Lizzie Green Lewis, opened a large box containing Allison's original quilts. One she'd already had in the shop. She lifted the blanket out and spread it on the table. The soft blue print design was mixed with ivories, spring greens and mauves.

"It's *bellissima*," Lizzie gasped. "Oh, *grazie*, Allison, *grazie*." She hugged her. Then went back to eye the quilt. "Did you make this?"

She nodded. "I didn't have time to make one with your colors. "It's called 'Forever and Always'." Allison's finger traced the linked circles. "It's one of my wedding quilt designs."

"I love it."

The tall, graceful hazel-eyed brunette was down to earth and Allison liked her right off. And a big surprise she got after Stefano had dropped them off this morning: the recent bride was very pregnant.

She also learned that Lizzie had been pregnant even before she'd met her husband, Jack. At the age of forty, she'd decided she wanted a baby and had been artificially inseminated.

"If I had known, I would have brought you a baby quilt."

Isabella showed up. "Then you would need two blankets."

"Twins?"

With a nod from Lizzie they all laughed.

The members of the Casali family Allison had met so far had been warm and welcoming to both her and Cherry. She hated to have to leave this wonderful place.

If only Alex could see what he was denying himself by not getting to know his siblings. He had two brothers and a sister. Even though he had a right to be angry, she refused to stay around while he continued to isolate himself from people. From a family he desperately needed in his life.

She turned to Isabella. "I had no idea there were all these new brides in the family. You were recently married, too."

She waved her hands. "How were you to know about all the weddings?" Alex's half-sister hugged her, too. "When the time comes, I will let you make me a quilt for my *bambino*."

Allison felt a tug on her heart, trying not to envy Lizzie's and Isabella's lives with their new husbands.

The promising future ahead of them. Something she doubted she would ever have with Alex, because he was still locked in his past.

Allison put on a smile. "Should I start on one now?"

Isabella winked. "I'll let you know. I wish you could meet Max before you leave." She gripped Allison's hands. "*Per favore*, say you'll stay a little while longer? Just ignore Alex and all the Casali men. They may be very handsome, but also stubborn."

Allison studied both women. Isabella, Alex's sister, and his cousin, Lizzie, were the ones who'd contacted Alex and his twin Angelo. Lizzie had been one of the few family members who knew of the twins' existence.

"Definitely stubborn," Lizzie agreed. "So you both need to convince Alex to stay."

Alex had come here. It was a good first step. Yet so far he'd refused to open up to the possibilities. Okay, so there'd been years of secrets and lies. She thought about the man who'd spent a lifetime closing himself off from everyone. But the Casalis were ready and more than willing to pull him and Angelo into the fold. He'd let her know last night that he didn't need her at all.

"I should go." She fought tears. "I still have to make reservations on a flight back to the States. I have a business to run back home and Cherry has her therapy."

Before Isabella could argue, Allison said, "You have to be the one to convince Alex to stay, and then you can get to know what a good man he is."

"If you leave, Alex will follow you." She shrugged. "I guess if he won't stay, then Max and I will just have to come to America. I've never been on a cattle ranch."

"You'd love it. And you can meet Tilda."

Isabella's eyes rounded. "Who is Tilda?"

"Years ago she was the ranch owner, then Alex bought it. At first, he kept her on as the housekeeper, then as the bookkeeper, and now she manages a lot of the ranch. But mostly, she's been Alex's family. She loves him as much as if he were her own son."

Tears filled Isabella's eyes. "I'm so glad he had someone in America. And you."

Alex doesn't want me, or at least he doesn't know it. Allison wanted to scream. She'd been foolish enough to involve him in her daughter's life, even come on this trip. Now, she had to get home before she did something truly foolish like confess her love for him.

"And now he has you and his family," she told Isabella.

Isabella started to speak but something caught her attention. Allison turned and saw Luca coming through the kitchen door, followed by Alex. He didn't look happy.

Her gaze couldn't capture enough of him. He was handsome in a strong, rugged way. His steel-gray eyes locked onto hers and she couldn't look away.

"Alex," Cherry cried and raised her arms. "You came to us."

Alex smiled at Cherry as he went to her and hugged her. Then he knelt down and they exchanged some quiet words. Luca waved for Isabella to come to him and quickly the room began to clear.

Before Alex's sister left her side, she said, "Seems someone is eager to talk to you." She took off and pushed Cherry out of the room.

Great. They were alone. Okay, maybe she was glad he was here.

"So you decided you couldn't handle it and are running out on me."

"No, you decided to push me away. And I didn't

want to argue anymore." She met his gaze. "I thought I could help you, Alex, but now I know it was a mistake that I came with you."

He turned away, raking his fingers through his hair. "No, it wasn't a mistake you came. And believe me you have helped me," he said as he looked at her. "More than you know. I was wrong to have acted the way I did last night, especially the way I treated you. I could blame it on the wine but—as I learned from my mother—that's just an easy excuse." His eyes held hers. "I had no right to take my anger and frustration out on you." His gaze softened. "And I swear, you'll never see me drink like that again."

She drew a deep breath and released it, inhaling his scent. It was doing crazy things to her common sense. "I'm glad to hear that." She glanced toward the table where Luca sat with Cherry. Her daughter was laughing. "You talked with Luca?"

"He showed up at the villa, and he wasn't going to leave until we talked." He fought to keep from smiling. "Seems the Casalis are known for their stubbornness."

"I think I heard that somewhere." She was surprised he would admit that. "So you and your father got a chance to talk. Did it help?"

Alex glanced away. "I wouldn't go as far to say that I'd ever call the man my father. I doubt that will ever happen. But I gave him my word that I'd stay a few days and meet all the family."

"Oh, Alex, that's wonderful news." She fought the tears, happy for him. She released a breath to compose herself, knowing that she was no longer needed here. "If you'll help get Cherry and me to Rome, we'll get a flight home."

"Why leave now, Allie?" He lowered his voice. "You're the one who convinced me to come—aren't you curious to see how things will turn out? At the least meet the rest of the Casalis."

Yes, she was curious about anything that concerned Alex, but she wasn't going to hang on, hoping things would turn out differently. "I have a business to run. Cherry has her therapy."

"We can call them, make another appointment. I'm only asking for a few days." He stepped closer. "You're running away, Allie."

She shook her head, but even she didn't believe it. "I'm not."

He leaned down and brushed a kiss over her lips. "You're scared. You made a mistake and trusted your husband and he let you and Cherry down." His gaze held hers. "I'm not him. I want to try and prove it to you. We need a chance to see where this leads. I won't let you down again. Don't desert me now."

"Oh, Alex." She had trouble keeping a clear head.

Alex cupped her face, praying that she would give him another chance. A lot of bad things had happened during his life, but seeing his father again cut into his heart. Allison had been his lifeline. He couldn't let her go.

"Then let me convince you." His mouth closed over hers, tasting the traces of her mint toothpaste. He drew her closer, holding her against him as if she would disappear. He couldn't let that happen, not now, and if he had the opportunity, not ever.

When he finally pulled back, he saw the want and need in her pretty emerald eyes. "A couple of days, Allie," he asked. "Give me a couple of days, that's all I ask. I promise you and Cherry will enjoy it."

She rewarded him with a smile. "My daughter is a pushover." She wrapped her arms around his neck. "It's me you have to convince, cowboy."

He smiled, too. "I'll do my best, ma'am." His head lowered to hers and he did as he promised.

CHAPTER TWELVE

DURING a pleasant lunch, Isabella convinced Alex to stay in town for the night so more of the Casalis could meet them. His persuasive younger sister even managed to talk him into a family dinner at Rosa's the next evening.

Before he could give her an answer, Isabella pulled out her phone and found them a nearby hotel. She then went along to help get them settled in their two-bedroom suite, and gave them ideas for sightseeing around Monta Correnti and the local countryside.

Alex hadn't spent any more time with his father, and Luca had disappeared into the kitchen. Allison worried about unresolved issues between the two men.

Once settled in the lovely hotel suite, Cherry had quickly fallen asleep after her busy day. Allison walked out of the bedroom. When she saw Alex talking with his cousin, Lizzie, she started to go back but he called to her.

"Allison, please join us." He stood and escorted her to the sitting area. "My cousin has been filling me in on the years I missed."

Allison put on a smile as she greeted Lizzie, then sat next to Alex on the sofa. At least she was happy that

Alex was willing to talk with his family about the past. "So you remember Alex and Angelo."

Lizzie sat with a protective hand over her rounded stomach. "I was telling Alex that I was only a few years older when they left." Sadness filled her eyes. "Yes, I remember a lot. For many years I was told never to mention the twins. And I was too young to not obey my mother."

Allison glanced at Alex to see his reaction. He didn't show any expression, but she could see his jaw tense.

She turned back to Lizzie and asked, "Why? Why all the secrecy?"

"I believe it was the shame. Families are supposed to stay together, but Luca couldn't support the boys. And my mother didn't help her brother at all. Maybe it was because of the circumstance of Luca's birth. Since he's William Valentine's son, there's always been friction between them. Even in business, they were competitive, and disagreed on how to run the restaurant. That's the reason Luca took his mother's maiden name, Casali, and the reason he opened Rosa."

She looked at Alex. "That's one of the reasons I came here tonight, to tell you something about my mother, Lisa Firenzi. You probably don't remember her."

Alex shook his head. "Only bits and pieces of my life here."

Lizzie nodded. "Here's a piece of news for you. Lisa is the real reason your papa had to send you and Angelo away. So any anger you have should be directed toward her."

More secrets had come out. Alex wasn't sure he wanted to deal with any more family turmoil. He took Allison's hand.

"Why is that?"

"It's no secret that my mother and Uncle Luca never got along. After Grandma Rosa died it got worse. Luca left the original family restaurant, Sorella, and started his own. When he opened Rosa's *ristorante* he worked all the time while trying to raise two boys on his own." She paused. "Your mother had already left him and gone back to America."

Knowing how selfish Cindy Daniels Casali was, he wasn't surprised.

"Luca knew he couldn't go on without help. He went to his sister and asked for a loan to get him through the difficult time." Lizzie glanced away. "Lisa turned him down and Luca had no other choice but to send you to your mother."

Alex stood and went to the window. "But why were we kept a secret?"

"I believe that was my mother's idea, too. She didn't want to bring shame onto the family, or be reminded that she had been a part of it." Lizzie stood and went to her cousin. "I only told you, Alex, because I don't want you to put all the blame on Luca. I know for a fact how much he missed you and Angelo."

Alex couldn't speak. So many emotions were stirred up.

"I should go." Lizzie stood. "My husband is waiting for me, and the *bambinos* are restless."

Alex froze. *"Bambinos?"*

She put on a smile and nodded. "Can you believe it? Twins. Boys." She wrapped her arms around him and hugged him. "I hope you're around to be in their lives," she whispered. "In my life, too. I'm glad you're home, cousin."

Lizzie released him, then gripped Allison's hand. "I hope to see more of you and Cherry. *Ciao*, Allison."

"I'll walk you down." Alex went with Lizzie to the door, but paused and went to Allison. He pulled her close. "I need to go out for a while. I can't ask you to wait up, but I'd like you to."

She nodded. "I'll be here."

Alex kissed her, wishing he could give her more, but he couldn't think about the future until he settled with the past.

The streets were almost empty at this late hour, but Alex found he enjoyed the peace and quiet. Even on the ranch, there'd always been the nagging voices from his past. Now, he knew about his past, where he'd come from. After he'd helped his cousin into her car, he'd started walking through the narrow streets, across the piazza, ending up at the restaurant. It wasn't a complete surprise; he needed to talk with Luca.

Finding the front door locked, he went around to the back and into the alley where there was an open door leading into the restaurant's kitchen. He stepped through the entry and saw the long stainless-steel counters stacked with dirty pans from the night's meals. Dishwashers were busy at the deep sinks, talking and working through the steam rising from the water.

How many years and how hard had his father worked to build this business? The long hours and days. Maybe that was where he and his brother got their work ethic. He'd never thought that he'd gotten much from his absent father. But although a world apart, they might have been similar in many respects. Life hadn't been easy for any of them.

The kitchen door opened and Luca appeared along with another employee, both speaking rapidly in Italian. When his father saw him, he sent the worker off.

"Alex." He went to him. "Is there a problem?"

"No. I was out for a walk and ended up here."

His father's expression relaxed, and a flash of Angelo came to mind. There were subtle similarities in their looks.

He motioned for Alex to follow him into the quiet dining room. "Monta Correnti must be very different than your ranch in Texas," Luca said.

Alex nodded. "Yes, but there are nice things about this area, too." He studied Luca. "Why didn't you tell me that Lisa wouldn't give you a loan so you could keep us here?"

He shrugged. "It doesn't excuse what I did. It was wrong to let you go. I still should have come to find you and Angelo. I should have known your mother…" He turned away. "She wasn't very maternal."

"That's an understatement."

Luca suddenly looked tired and older than his years as he sank into a chair. "I did send money to her for the first few years. I even called. Then I lost track of you both. I should have tried harder, I know. Cindy made it difficult. I'll always regret that I never came to get you."

"So will I."

"I'm sorry, Alex. I'm sorry I wasn't there for you." Luca stared at him for a long time. "A day never went by that I didn't think about you and Angelo. You both were in my mind, in my heart, always."

Alex glanced away, not liking the sudden heaviness in his chest. "There are some things I remember about living here. A small room that I shared with Angelo. Who called me *uccellino*?"

"Little bird." Luca's smile brightened but Alex saw tears in his eyes. "It was a story I read to you and your brother. But you, Alessandro, carried the book around all the time, begging me to read it again and again. I still have the book along with photos of you and Angelo. If you like I could show you."

Alex wasn't sure he could handle any more right now. He shook his head. "Maybe another time. I need to get back to Allison and Cherry."

Luca nodded. "You are a lucky man to have two special ladies in your life."

Yes, he was lucky. He hoped they would be patient enough to wait for him to figure it out.

Allison stood at the window in the bedroom she shared with Cherry. She couldn't go to sleep, not as long as Alex was out there. As much as she wanted to help, he needed time and some space to take it all in. And knowing Alex as she did, he had to do it on his own.

She glanced at Cherry asleep in the bed. The one thing that had made this trip worthwhile had been the change in her daughter. All the affection and attention she'd gotten from the Casalis had been incredible. Allison was also concerned about the letdown for her daughter when they had to go back to Texas, move back into their small apartment.

Allison wasn't foolish enough to believe in fairy tales. Not anymore. She'd faced too many challenges on her own to believe that someone would come charging in to rescue her. Her disastrous marriage and Cherry's accident had made her stronger; she had learnt to rely on herself.

What part of Alex's life they fit into, she wasn't sure,

but she wasn't going to be his charity case just because he had a lot of money. She loved him too much to let that happen.

A soft knock sounded on the door, but before she could answer it Alex poked his head inside. He nodded once in her direction as he walked to the bed and pulled the covers a little higher over Cherry. Studying the child for a moment, he brushed back her hair. Even in the dim light, Allison could see Alex cared about her daughter.

He glanced at her and motioned for her to come with him. Allison took a calming breath and followed him out. She stepped into the sitting area just as he pulled her into his arms.

Alex didn't wait for her protest, his need for her won out and he bent his head and his mouth covered hers. Her lips were warm and she tasted cool. With a groan, she lifted her fingers to his hair as her tongue slid over his. He liked her eagerness. The way she touched him, the way her breasts pressed against his chest. She tasted like everything he'd ever wanted and needed, but spent his life trying to stay away from. Until now.

He finally drew back, working to catch his breath enough to speak. "You waited up for me."

"You asked me to," she whispered.

He smiled, wanting her desperately. He lowered his head and rained kisses along her jaw and neck, feeling the slow, heavy need coursing through his blood. "You taste good. Really good."

"So do you," she whispered in between nibbles on his mouth, making him more aroused than ever. He plunged his fingers into her hair, deepening the kiss, wanting to sink into her so far, there was no separation between them. Instead, he drew back, and released her.

"I better slow down before I break my promise to you." He knew this trip to Italy was supposed to be hands off. But when she looked at him with those big eyes he nearly lost it.

He turned away. "I came from seeing my father."

Allison looked surprised. "At the restaurant?"

He nodded. "We talked about what Lizzie told me tonight. He wouldn't let his sister take all the blame." He went on to tell her about the photos and his childhood storybook. "Although I can't think of him as a father, I know now I want a relationship with him and the rest of my family here."

Her eyes flooded with tears. "Oh, Alex, I'm happy for you."

He blinked. "I don't know if happy is the word I'd use. I've never considered myself a family man, and now I seem to have a rather large one whether I like it or not. And you've had a lot to do with that."

She shook her head. "Your sister, Isabella, was the one who contacted you." She glanced away. "Now, you have to stay awhile and meet the rest of the Casalis. Cherry and I should go back to Texas. That will give you time to visit without having to worry about us." She put some distance between them. "I still have our tickets to return to the States. I can make reservations tomorrow."

Alex swore. "No. Don't leave, Allie." He reached for her. Heat surged through him and his lips caressed hers.

He raised his head, but didn't release her. "I'll fly the damn therapist over here," he murmured. "Whatever you want or need to keep you here. I want you with me." He touched her face. "I need you, Allie. If you believe anything, believe that you and Cherry are important to me." He tilted her head toward his. "I don't want to be separated from you even for a little while."

Allison couldn't think rationally right now. Not when she was in Alex's arms. When it came to this man she hadn't been able to think since that first day when he had ridden up to her on his horse. She wanted this man like no other.

"Oh, Alex, I don't want to be away from you, either."

"God, Allie. You say things like that and I won't be able to stop."

She raised up and kissed him. "Then don't. Don't walk away from me again."

"I couldn't leave here if the place was on fire." He swung her up into his arms and carried her into his bedroom. The place was dimly lit as he placed her next to the bed. Then he captured her mouth and she sank into him, her lips parting under his. She wanted to lose herself in him, if only for this one time. She pulled back and reached for the bedside lamp.

"Leave it on," he urged. "I don't want to miss any of this night."

Alex let out a long breath. He stepped forward and began to remove her clothes, starting with her peasant-style blouse. With a shaky hand, he tugged on the elastic neck and pulled it down her torso, exposing her bra. With her help, he continued the job, pushing her top along with her skirt until they lay in a pool on the floor. She stepped out, leaving her in only a pair of lacy panties and bra.

He stood back and yanked off his shirt, then tossed it aside. Somehow he managed to get his boots and his trousers off. "There's not going to be any more hesitation, Allie. This night is for us. Only us."

He reached for her, drawing her against him as he kissed her once, twice, soon losing count. He backed her to the bed until she was lying down on the mattress.

He paused, leaning over her. "God, Allie, I want you. For so long."

She smiled at him and cupped his face. "I don't need words, Alex, I need you."

"You got me, Allie. You got me."

She wrapped her arms around his neck, tugging him closer. She wanted this memory to keep forever. She pressed her lips to his and whispered, "Make it a night to remember."

His mouth closed over hers and he proceeded to fulfill his promise.

The next morning, Allison awoke in her own bed for obvious reasons. Of course it hadn't erased the incredible night she'd spent with Alex, but she'd needed to be there for Cherry. She wasn't ready for her daughter's questions, either.

The one thing that dampened her spirits was when she came out for breakfast and found Alex gone. Again. Yet, she had no right to feel disappointed. There hadn't been any promises. During their night together, Alex had made her feel incredibly special, but he'd never spoken a word about love. And she knew he might never do so.

It was something she had to be prepared to live with.

She glanced at her daughter while she ate her breakfast. There had been so many positive changes in her in the last month. Alex was a big part of that and the child had become very attached to him. What would happen when they returned home?

"Mommy, is Alex gonna live here?"

Where had she heard that? "Honey, I don't know, but he has a ranch back home."

"Yeah, someone has to take care of all the horses and Maisie." She ate a piece of cut fruit. "But his daddy lives here. And Luca wants Alex to stay. He said so." Cherry looked at her. "I wish I had a daddy, too."

Allison froze. This was the first time Cherry had mentioned her father since before the accident. "I wish I could give you one, honey. But remember we talked about this—Jack lives in Arizona."

"And he doesn't want a little girl," she said matter-of-factly.

It was the truth, but Allison wished it would be different for her child. "But I want a little girl, one just like you." She got up and came around to hug her. "I love you, Cherry."

"I love you, too, Mommy." She pulled back. "I wish I had Alex for my daddy."

Allison tried not to react. "I know he's been good to you. He might not be your daddy but he can be a friend. He'll let you ride Maisie."

That finally made her daughter smile. "I miss her, and Tilda and Brian."

"Well, we'll be going home soon. But remember, we'll be going home to our place in town." She raised a hand to stop her daughter's protest. "I have to run the shop. And you have therapy, so you can walk again. For that to happen, we need to go back."

Suddenly the door to the suite opened and Alex strolled in. "*Buon giorno*, ladies," he called, and came to the table. Leaning over, he kissed Cherry's cheek, then Allison's surprised mouth.

"Hi, Alex," Cherry said. "We didn't know where you went."

He frowned. "You didn't? I left your mother a note."

"What note?" Allison asked, unable to turn away. The man looked too good the first thing in the morning, in jeans especially. Of course, he wasn't bad at night either.

"I didn't want to wake you, so I left it on your night-stand to tell you I was going out for a while." When he headed toward her bedroom, she got up and followed. He pointed to her side of the bed. "I put it right there." With further searching, he found it on the floor. "Here it is."

Allison took it and read it.

> Allie,
> I hope I made your night memorable, because it was for me. Have a special errand to run this morning. See you in a few hours.
>   Alex.

She felt her heart race. "Oh, Alex. Last night was wonderful for me, too, but we have to be realistic about this. It's going to have to end sometime."

He drew her into his arms. "I'm not very good at this, Allie. I've been alone a long time. Then you and Cherry came into my life and bowled me over and confused the hell out of me."

"Is that good?"

He placed a finger on her lips to stop her. "You and Cherry are important to me." He pulled her back into his arms and took her mouth in a soul-searing kiss, trying to convince her not to give up on him. "You stood by me, helping me get through this mess with my family. You should have given up on me long ago."

She blinked. "I'm glad we helped you."

"In more ways than you'll ever know." He blew out a breath. "I'm not where I need to be yet. But being with you last night made me realize that I don't want to let you go. I want—"

"Hey, what about me?" Cherry called. They broke apart just as the child pushed her chair into the doorway.

Allison turned to Alex. "Just so you know, she has to come first. I don't want her hurt anymore. It's not just you and me, it's the three of us."

He smiled. "I wouldn't want it any other way."

An hour later they drove into Naples for some sightseeing and shopping. Alex took the girls into an exclusive shop. With a promise from the boutique owner to take care of them, he sat back and watched the show.

Allison reluctantly tried on dresses, arguing that she didn't need anything. But Alex refused to budge and she finally went back into a dressing room and came out in a soft pink print with narrow straps and a full skirt that was short enough to show off her shapely legs. Oh, yes, he was enjoying this.

After purchasing two dresses he knew Allison loved along with a pair of sandals, they went on to a children's store where Cherry got her turn.

Who would have thought that the Texas rancher would be sitting in a too-small chair, waiting for his favorite little girl to try on a dress?

When Allison wheeled Cherry out in a pretty blue party dress and they were both smiling, he realized he was having the time of his life. He wanted them both with him always.

"Do you like this one, Alex?" Cherry asked.

"I think you're the prettiest girl ever."

She blushed, then said, "No, my mom is the prettiest girl. Do you think she's pretty, too?"

Alex looked at Allison. Yes, she was. That auburn hair and those green eyes had gotten to him a long time ago.

"Yes, she is." He finally tore his gaze away. "And you look like her."

After paying for the purchase, they walked out of the store in search of gifts to take home for Tilda and Brian. Instead, they ended up in a toy store after Cherry fell in love with a doll in the window. That was all it took for Alex to go inside and hand over his credit card to the shop owner.

On the way out, Allison leaned close to him and whispered, "You know you don't have to buy her everything. You already won her over the day you introduced her to her first horse."

He cared so much for Cherry, and it upset him that he couldn't give her a miracle so she could walk. One thing was for sure, he'd do whatever it took to get her on her feet. He would give her the best of everything.

"How about her mother?" He locked in on her mesmerizing gaze. "Have I won her over?" He meant it as a joke, but then she hesitated and he found he was eager for her answer.

She only smiled. "Let me get back to you on that."

CHAPTER THIRTEEN

By LATE afternoon they had arrived back at the hotel so they could dress for the Casali family dinner. Cherry had fallen asleep during the ride, so she was rested for the party.

Alex got ready in twenty minutes. Being with Allison and Cherry, enjoying the day, he'd almost forgotten he had to meet up with the rest of Casali clan tonight. He hadn't run away from anything since he'd been a hungry street kid in New York. Now, he had to fight that old urge. It was time to deal with the past.

He walked into the sitting area and called his brother. He wanted to give it one more try to convince Angelo to come to Italy, or at least tell him what he'd discovered about the family.

He soon learned that nothing was going to sway his twin brother. "I guess I'm not as forgiving as you are, Alex," Angelo said. "Nothing changed the fact that our old man still shipped us off to the States."

"That's true, but things are different now. He isn't the only one who's involved. There are two brothers and a sister who knew nothing about us."

Alex turned when he heard the bedroom door open, and Allison appeared pushing Cherry into the room.

He got a warm feeling inside seeing their bright smiles. He managed to return it before he turned his attention back to the phone call. "They are family, too," Alex told his brother.

There was silence on the other end.

Alex continued, "Okay, I get the message. I'm staying for another few days, but those arrangements can be changed if you decide to make the trip. I can send my plane."

"Thanks for the offer, but don't count on me," Angelo said. "Look, have a great time in Italy. I gotta go, talk to you when you get back. *Ciao*." Then there was silence as his brother hung up.

Alex closed his phone. He wasn't going to let Angelo ruin his mood. He'd made a promise to himself that he'd at least meet the rest of the family and show his special ladies a nice evening. After that he could pack up, go back to Texas and move on with his life.

He went to them, eyeing Allison in the rose-pink print sundress with thin straps and fitted on the top, showing off her tiny waist and her other assets. The fabric looked soft, touchable. So did she. "You both look *bellissima*."

Allison blushed. "Thank you."

"That means beautiful, Mommy," Cherry said proudly. "Thank you, Alex, for my pretty dress, too."

He leaned down and kissed the child's cheek. "You're welcome, darlin'. Does this mean you'll never wear jeans again when we get back home?"

"Yes, I will, 'cause I want to ride Maisie. I miss her and Tilda and Brian."

"And they all miss you, too," he assured her. "We'll be home in a few days. But right now we have a party to go to."

* * *

Thirty minutes later they arrived at the restaurant and Alex escorted Allison and Cherry inside. Right off he was intimidated by the number of people there. It seemed they were all related to him either by blood or by marriage.

"Isn't it wonderful?" Allison said. "Look at all the family you have, Alex."

Before he could say anything, his father came up to him. "*Buona sera*, Alex and Allison." He shook Alex's hand and kissed Allison's cheeks. Then he bent down and did the same to Cherry. "I can't tell you how wonderful it is that you came tonight. There are so many who want to see you."

Alex glanced at Allison. "I told you I'd be here, but you neglected to tell me about the size of the group."

Luca's smile faded. "Yes, you kept your word. My only hope is that you will stay in touch with your new family."

Alex felt that tug again toward a man he'd never gotten the chance to know. The man he'd never called father. Luca was getting up in years and he hadn't had an easy life. Alex glanced away. None of them had. "I expect Isabella will see to that."

Luca smiled again. "*Sì*, your sister works hard to see that the Casalis stay together," he said, and then added, "And tonight, we celebrate because we are together."

A waiter came by with glasses of champagne. His father began handing them out. Once he got the crowd's attention, he held up his glass. "I have been blessed with so much over the years, but having one of my sons return home is a prayer answered. *Bentornato*, Alessandro. Welcome back." He lifted his glass higher. "*Salute.*"

After the toast Allison tried to stand back as several

family members came over to greet them. It was over-whelming with all the hugs and kisses. Her once-shy daughter was eating up the attention. Allison loved watching Cherry blossom, but couldn't help but wonder how she would handle going back home.

Alex reached for Allison's hand, drawing her back to him. "Don't desert me," he said. "You're the one who convinced me having family was wonderful."

She smiled. "I still believe that. You're a lucky man, Alex."

He leaned down, his eyes locked on hers. "I know that." He brushed his mouth over hers. "If we were alone, I'd be showing you how much."

A shiver shot through Allison, but before she could answer Isabella made her way through the crowd, bringing her husband with her. The perfect description of the man was tall, dark and handsome. She introduced her new groom, Maximilliano Di Rossi. Even the scars beneath the stubble on his chin didn't detract from his good looks.

"We first met when I was trespassing on the grounds of his palazzo," Isabella confessed.

"I take it he didn't have you arrested," Alex said.

Max pulled his wife closer. "My life would have been simpler if I had." He sent Isabella a heated look. "But not nearly as wonderful."

Finally Isabella looked at Alex. "I was searching for Monta Rosa basil. It's the secret ingredient for Rosa's special tomato sauce. You need to know this since it's part of your heritage, too."

"I guess I have a lot to learn. Maybe I should teach you about beef cattle. Max, you will have to bring my sister to Texas."

His sister looked surprised. "Are you inviting us?"

Alex wasn't sure what he was doing. He normally didn't like people invading his space, until a pretty redhead had come into his life. "The A Bar A is a big place. With the guest ranch, we have plenty of room for everyone."

Lizzie appeared and introduced her husband, Jack. And soon another couple. It was his brother Valentino and an attractive brunette.

Alex eyed Italy's one-time playboy and thrill seeker. Now married, he seemed to stay close to home and family.

He extended a hand. "We didn't get much of a chance to talk the other night. I'm Alex. I hear we're brothers."

A few heartbeats passed, then Valentino took the offered hand. They shook. "Are you sure you want to claim this crazy *famiglia*?"

"It seems it's all I have."

They all laughed and Alex realized he was having a good time. Valentino drew forward a small woman with dark brown hair and jade eyes. "Alex, this is my wife, Clara. Clara, this is my long-lost brother from America, Alex Casali."

"It's nice to meet you, Clara. This is Allison Cole and her daughter, Cherry." He pointed down toward the child at the table.

"It's nice to meet you," Allison said.

"It's a pleasure."

Alex turned back to Valentino. "I apologize for leaving so abruptly the other night."

Valentino nodded. "It's understandable. This family can be overwhelming," he said, glancing at Luca. "But very protective. I'm happy you came back to visit. You've made our papa happy."

Alex studied the one-time race-car driver, who had recently married his childhood sweetheart. He'd also given her a kidney. "What about you? Are you happy about my return?"

"Yes, I am." He smiled and hugged his wife next to him. "I have family, and I'm married to the love of my life." He glanced at his father. "And we have some wonderful news, too. Clara is pregnant."

Cheers went up in the room as Luca hugged Valentino and Alex found he was a little jealous. "Congratulations," Alex said.

"Thank you. Since you're going to have a niece or nephew, you'll need to come and visit more often."

Once again Luca raised a glass. "We have another generation beginning."

His father turned around where an older woman appeared in the doorway. The crowd hushed as she locked her dark gaze on Alex. He'd never seen her before. She was attractive, her age somewhere between fifty and sixty. She had black hair, cut in a long, straight style that brushed her shoulders. Although their coloring was different, there was a family resemblance to Luca. Then recognition hit him.

Lisa Firenzi.

Luca lifted his glass once more to the woman. "Let's hope they do better than we did, dear *sorella*."

With a nod, Lisa walked in as regal as a queen, and came directly to Alex.

"Alex, this is your aunt Lisa Firenzi. Lisa, your nephew, Alex."

She smiled but it didn't reach her eyes. "*Ciao*, Alessandro. It's good to have you home. It's been too long."

He tensed, knowing she'd had a lot to do with his disappearance, too. "*Ciao*, Lisa."

The room remained quiet as attention zeroed in on them. "I'm sorry," Lisa said, "I was out of town when you arrived." She tried to smile again, but it didn't work. "As you can see, I'm not exactly the favorite person here." She took a breath. "But I had to come. For you. To apologize for my part in you and your brother leaving Monta Correnti. I had no idea that it would turn out as it did."

Alex nodded, but he wasn't sure about her sincerity. "I'm not here to place blame, Lisa. Too many years have passed to rehash all the wrong. I'm here because I wanted to meet my sister and brothers and long-lost cousins."

He felt Allison reach for his hand, giving him courage. "So let's enjoy this evening."

"Yes," Luca added as he took his place next to his sister. "It's time we put the mistakes of the past aside. We have much more to be grateful for. Your grandmother, Rosa Casali Firenzi, worked hard to keep her family together." He handed Lisa a glass of wine. "We have another generation starting, sister. With that there is always hope that things will be better.

"Everyone raise your glasses for all the blessings bestowed on our family." He raised his glass over his head and looked at Alex. "*Al famiglia.*"

Alex lifted his and repeated the words that had come to mean something to him since being in Italy. Could he forget the past? No, not all of it, but he knew now that he wanted to look ahead to a future. And not just for him and his brother. Now he knew he had room in his heart for more. He looked at Allison and Cherry. He wanted them in his future.

* * *

Hours later, after a delicious meal and far too much wine, Allison was exhausted, and so was Cherry. It had been a long day and night, and her daughter needed to be in bed. If they were just going back to the hotel, she would go alone, and leave Alex here to spend more time with his family, but they were going back to the villa tonight.

Allison thought back to last night and sharing Alex's bed. She wanted to think they'd grown closer with all the positive attention he'd given her, and Cherry. The big question was what would happen once they returned home? Would he give them a chance?

She glanced around the large room, but didn't see Alex. She asked around and a waiter directed her out to the patio area. She came to the iron gate where she saw Alex sitting with Luca. Seeing that they were deep in conversation, she turned to leave when she heard her name mentioned.

It was Alex who said, "It was Allison who convinced me to come here."

"Then I am grateful to her," Luca said. "She's a special woman."

There was a pause, and Allison found herself holding her breath, hoping for Alex's confession of his undying love.

"And she's a special mother," Alex answered. "When we get back, I plan to help with Cherry's treatment. She's going to have the best of everything. I owe them that much."

Allison didn't want his gratitude. She knew Alex cared about her and Cherry, but would he share the most important part of himself? His heart. She turned and walked back inside. It was time for her to go home.

* * *

Alex was surprised to find he was relaxed as he talked with Luca. He wanted some time getting to know his father.

"I believe you have picked the perfect woman in Allison," his father said.

"How do you know I've picked her?"

Luca smiled knowingly. "Your face gives you away. Your eyes follow her around a room. She makes you smile. And the child, she's in your heart, too."

Since adulthood, Alex had had few doubts about getting what he wanted. Whenever he set his sights on something, he usually got it, except when it came to relationships. He knew he didn't want to live without her. "But it's hard for me to trust my heart."

"She is your heart."

Twenty minutes later, they said their goodbyes to family. Alex pulled Isabella aside. "How is the restaurant really doing?"

His sister glanced away. "It's not in the best of shape, but our cousin, Scarlett, is returning from Australia. She's a financial advisor and is willing to help with Rosa."

"Do you trust her to turn things around?"

Isabella nodded. "We talked a lot at Lizzie's wedding. She has some good ideas about bringing tourism to this area."

Alex was troubled as to why he cared. "If you need anything, you call me." He pulled out a business card. "For anything."

His sister took the card and hugged him. "Oh, Alex, I'm so happy I finally got to meet you."

He returned the hug. "I'm glad, too."

"So will I get a wedding invitation so I have an excuse to come see you in Texas?"

"You don't need an excuse to visit."

Her smiled widened. "Maybe then you'll be able to meet Cristiano." She frowned. "He's gone through a bad time lately with his injuries, but he's getting better. He'll be sorry he missed you, but it wasn't possible for him to be here."

"I'd like to meet him," he said, hearing about the heroics of the firefighter. "And maybe by then Angelo will come around, too."

Isabella smiled. "And then we'll all be one big happy family."

Alex smiled, too. "Maybe that's a little too much to hope for." He glanced again at Allison. He'd settled for his own small family of three.

Earlier that evening, Alex had asked the hotel to pack up everything and put it in the town car so that they could head back to Monte Vista tonight.

What he wanted couldn't wait one more day. But what surprised him was how distant Allison was suddenly. Okay, his family was overwhelming, and she was probably exhausted from their long day, but he'd hoped to continue a private celebration with just the two of them.

Alex carried the sleeping Cherry into the villa and started up the stairs.

"We could have taken the elevator," Allison said, following him.

"I've lifted calves that were heavier. And I don't mind carrying this sweet package."

"And I like you to carry me," Cherry said in her sleepy voice.

"Don't wake up too much," her mother warned. "Because you're going to bed."

"I had fun at the party, Alex. I wish I had a grandpa and aunts and uncles like you do."

He hoped she meant that. "They all adore you, too. So maybe they'll adopt you."

They went through the suite door, continuing on to the bedroom where he laid her down on the mattress in the alcove.

"What does 'dopt mean?" Cherry asked.

Alex thought a moment as Allison went to the dresser and took out pajamas. "Let's see, it means that someone loves a child so much that they want that child to come live with them forever."

The girl's eyes rounded. "I wish you'd 'dopt me."

"Cherry Ann Cole, you shouldn't say that."

"But, Mommy, I want Alex to be my daddy."

Allison's face flamed. "It's time you were asleep. Alex, if you'll excuse us."

He didn't move. Instead he leaned down and whispered, "I want to adopt you, too. For now keep it a secret. Okay?" The child smiled and nodded. Then he placed a kiss on her cheek and left.

He touched Allison's arm. "I'd like to talk with you."

She sighed. "I'm really tired, Alex. Couldn't it wait until morning?"

"Five minutes, Allie. That's all I ask."

When she nodded, he left and went straight out onto the balcony. He couldn't wait to make his feelings known to her.

After pouring a glass of sparkling water, he took out his cell phone and called Brian at the ranch. The time difference made it hours earlier in Texas. After getting updates, he gave his foreman an assignment to find an architect to draw up plans for a therapy room that included an indoor pool. He had to prove to Allison he was going to be the man for her and her daughter. He loved them both.

Allison appeared in the doorway. "What is it you need to talk about?"

She was still being distant.

"Us."

She blew out a breath. "Is there an, 'us', Alex? I mean, aren't I just a companion on this trip? Isn't that why you brought us?"

"Maybe at first, but not anymore."

She tried to look unapproachable but he saw her nervousness. "What changed?"

"Me. You changed me. You and that little girl in the other room."

"I don't want you to feel obligated to us."

"What makes you think that?"

"I heard you with Luca. You told him you owed us. You don't owe us anything, Alex. And we don't need your pity. I came here with you to Italy of my own free will. If you think I came to your bed last night because I felt I owed you, then you're sadder than I thought." She turned to leave and he stopped her.

"Hold it right there, Allie. You had your say, now I get mine." He took a breath, then released it, trying to refrain from shaking her. "First of all, you didn't hear all the conversation. I said I owed you because without you I wouldn't have opened up to my family." He raised a hand. "I'm not about to call Luca Dad, but we are talking now. And if you hadn't convinced me to come in the first place, I would have never met the rest of the

Casalis." He took a step toward her. "You did that, Allie. You made me feel things. For the first time you made me feel joy."

"Oh, Alex," she whispered.

He placed a finger over her lips as his gaze met hers. "I don't want to go back to my solitary life. I need you, Allie. If you believe anything, believe that. You and Cherry are important to me. More important than I've ever let anyone become." He cupped her face in his hands. "I never want to leave you or Cherry. So understand I will never abandon that little girl." He nodded toward the bedroom. "I love her too much."

Tears filled Allison's eyes.

"I love her mother, too. Oh, God, Allie. I love you." He took her mouth in a swift kiss, trying to convince her that he was worth the chance. "Just give me time to prove that I'm the man you need. To prove that I can make us a family."

"Oh, Alex, don't you know? You're everything I've ever wanted. I love you, too. I don't want you to change anything." She smiled. "But I could use some more convincing."

His head lowered and his mouth covered hers. He drew her against his body, trying to get her as close as possible. Things were beginning to get out of hand when he knew he had to pull back, for now.

"Hold that thought," he told her, and hurried off to his room. He dug through his suitcase, found what he needed and returned to the balcony.

His heart raced as he looked at the woman he loved so much. "Yesterday morning when I left and you wondered where I went—I knew after spending the night with you in my arms, making love to you, I couldn't let you go. Ever."

He pulled out the small, blue velvet box and opened it, revealing the pear-shaped diamond, surrounded by smaller emeralds.

"Oh, Alex."

"If it's not to your liking, we can shop for something else when we get home."

She shook her head. "It's beautiful. Perfect."

He relaxed a little. "The emeralds reminded me of your eyes. I love your eyes."

"And I love this ring, because you chose it."

With a smile, he went down on one knee. "Allison Cole, I love you with all my heart. Will you marry me and will you and Cherry come live on the ranch with me?"

Allison was choked with emotion but managed to nod. He slipped the ring on her finger. The solitary diamond sparkled up at her.

"Oh, Alex. I love you. Yes. Yes, I'll marry you."

He stood and pulled her to him. First he kissed her cheek, the corner of her mouth and then her lips, savoring the special moment with her. When he finally released her and said, "I want Cherry, too. I want her to be my daughter. I'll do right by her, Allie. She'll have only the best of everything. I'm building her a therapy room at the ranch. We'll go see the best doctors."

Allison placed her finger against his mouth and he captured her hand. "She's going to have the best, Alex. She'll have you as her father."

"No, I'm the lucky one. I have you, Allie, and as a bonus I have Cherry, too." He placed a kiss on her nose. "We're all lucky. Do you want to get married here or Texas?"

"I think we should get married at home, in Texas." She kissed him. "But that doesn't mean we can't start the celebration in Italy."

He swung her up in his arms. "Whatever the lady wants."

"You. I'll always choose you."

Alex paused as the overwhelming feelings swelled in his chest so he could barely speak. "I want to give you and Cherry everything."

"You've given us the most important thing. You." She touched her mouth to his. "That, and your love, is all a girl could ever want."

"And you're giving me what I've always wanted: love and family."

EPILOGUE

TEN months later Allison stood in the new therapy room Alex had had built as soon as they returned from Italy. The structure—including an indoor pool—was located behind the main building at the Hidden Hills Guest Ranch, which was now known as Cherry's Camp.

The reason for the close proximity was to change the place into a ranch for disabled children. Children who otherwise couldn't have a vacation. Now, they could come to summer camp to ride and be with other kids, even continue their therapy. The camp would have two therapists on staff during the summer. It was due to open in a few weeks. With enrollment filled to capacity, there were already plans for expansion by adding a gymnasium for even more activities.

Tilda was in charge of it all and there was a minimal fee for the week of vacation. Alex could afford to be generous.

"Have they started yet?"

Allison turned and smiled as her husband of the last several months came into the room. He moved with that easy gait that she'd come to love, along with how he looked in a pair of jeans and a cocked cowboy hat.

She rose up on her toes and kissed him. "Do you think Cherry would do anything without you here to see her?"

"I hope not," he said, frowning. "But she's getting pretty independent since she's started school. I love it, but I hate it at the same time. She's my little girl."

Allison knew the feeling. "Oh, Alex, you're the one who's helped make her strong so she can handle this, and make her believe she can reach for goals. From the first day when you picked her up off the ground she knew you'd be there for her."

Alex was having trouble holding onto his emotions, especially when it came to his girls. "It took a lot longer for me to win over her mother."

Allison smiled and patted her rounded stomach. "I'd say you were pretty convincing. Papa."

He loved the endearment she'd called him since the morning they'd read the positive pregnancy test results. He glanced around for a chair. "Shouldn't you be sitting down?"

"That's all I've been doing." She let him lead her to the row of chairs along the wall of the large workout room and sat down. "I'm pregnant like millions of other women."

"But they aren't my wife, and aren't carrying my son and daughter." He drew a breath. They hadn't planned adding to their family quite yet, but nature had had other ideas when he and Allie had stolen some time alone and gone riding to their special place. He was crazy about the idea.

"I still can't believe it. Twins."

She gave him a sideways glance. "We're going to have to rename your special place Double Trouble."

He grinned. "Or Double Delight."

She raised an eyebrow. "Oh, I like that. Just so you know when the time comes you'll be a terrific dad." She leaned back against him. "Just like you are to Cherry."

For years, Alex had doubted that he'd ever have enough to give to have a life with someone. Then Allison had come into his life. She'd helped him heal his past hurts and given him hope for the future. She'd got him to talk about his childhood, to share even the worst times. She cried over the twin boys who'd been left alone, who were made to feel that no one loved them. Alex knew that even during that time, he had Angelo. They had each other. Now, he had family in Italy, and his wife, daughter and two more babies on the way.

"Are you sure you're not doing too much?" He stroked his hand up and down her arm. "I mean with your quilt shop and the cable show."

It had taken time and a good lawyer, but Allison had got out of the legal agreement with her ex-husband. It had cost Alex some money, but it was worth it. Jack Hudson had no more control over Allison's life.

She smiled at him. "*Quilt Allie* is on once a week. And I'm seated most of the time. And soon Jenny will be taking over."

Alex had been happy when Jenny Collins had eagerly agreed to work on the show with Allison. The teacher was a natural for television. What she lacked in expertise, she made up for in enthusiasm. The audience loved her. Her biggest fan was Brian. The two had been seeing each other since they met at the first quilting retreat.

"At least she's moved to Kerry Springs after the first of the year. Maybe that will help with her relationship with Brian."

Alex cringed. "They're doing just fine without our help. If the two want to work it out, they'll find a way."

Those green eyes lit up and he knew she was planning something. "I just want them to be happy, too."

"They don't seem unhappy to me." Alex shook his head. "Besides, Brian will be pretty busy building a house on the east end of the ranch."

Allison gasped again. "You did what I suggested. You gave him part of the ranch."

"A few acres aren't even noticeable on this spread. Besides, he's earned them. And now, since he's bought a partnership in the cattle operation, I don't have to be away so much."

Her eyes widened. "Careful, Alex, you'll lose that tough-guy image."

"As if I ever fooled you," he said, happy she'd seen through it all.

"You have a big heart, Alessandro Casali. And I love that you chose to share it with me."

He kissed her. "We chose each other."

He pulled her against him, enjoying just being with her, sharing things. "I talked to Luca earlier," he mentioned. They'd kept in touch since the trip to Italy. "I asked him to come for a visit after the babies are born. And somehow I'm going to get Angelo here, too."

Allison raised her head up from his shoulder and looked at him. "I don't think I could love you more than I do at this moment." She placed her hand on his jaw. "I repeat, you are a nice man. And I love you."

"I love you, too."

He gave her a lingering kiss, but it still had his pulse pounding and heart racing. He pulled back and smiled. "Later," he promised as Tilda came through the door.

"Am I in time to see Cherry?" she asked.

"She hasn't even come in yet," Alex said.

The older woman rubbed her hands together. "Good, I didn't want to miss this."

Soon Brian and Jenny showed up. They had big smiles on their faces as Brian shared the news about plans for his house.

Alex watched the women chat away and he realized they might not be blood, but they were all his family. They cared for each other.

"Here she comes," Tilda announced as therapist, Kate Boyer, escorted Cherry into the room. Alex's daughter wasn't in a wheelchair much these days. As often as possible, she got around with her braces and crutches.

Nearly six years old now, Cherry Casali worked hard during therapy sessions. Alex had given her an incentive, too. The promise of her own horse. For months the girl had worked all the time and barely complained about it. They always knew that Cherry might never walk on her own and if she did, she would probably have a limp.

A lot of the time, Alex was in on his daughter's workouts, but the last few weeks she'd banned everyone from the therapy room. Until today when she'd summoned them all here.

"Hi, Mommy and Daddy. And everybody," she called. "Stay there. I want to show you something."

She made her way to the parallel bars and eased down in a chair where Kate helped her remove her braces. Alex's heart nearly stopped and Allison gripped his hand tightly.

He watched the strain on Cherry's face as she reached

for the outside of the bar and pulled herself up with one hand. Once standing she looked across the room, her gaze locked on him.

He held onto Allison's hand and whispered the words, "You can do it, *uccellino*."

It seemed as if everyone held their breath as Cherry took that first step, then another. Tilda gasped and Allison began to cry and he felt his own tears gathering as their daughter continued the hardest journey of her short life. He couldn't sit there any longer. He got up and walked to the end of the railing.

"You can do it, Cherry," he repeated. "I'll be here for you."

She smiled and continued each slow step until she made it to the end and stood in front of him. "See, Daddy, I did it. I did it."

He swung her up into his arms, and hugged her to him. "I always knew you could."

Allison joined them, giving her daughter a kiss as whistles and cheers broke out in the room.

"Don't cry, Mommy," Cherry said. "You're supposed to be happy."

"Oh, I am, sweetheart. You've made me so very happy."

Alex knew that Allison could finally move on from the guilt, stop blaming herself for her daughter's accident. This had been the one thing he couldn't help her with. But Cherry had.

"Do I get my horse now, Daddy?"

Allison looked at him, wiping her tears. "Looks like she won and you have to pay up, Casali."

"It's my pleasure to pay off this bet."

Cherry hugged him. "You're the best daddy and mommy ever."

Alex looked at Allison and Cherry, and his chest tightened with love and pride. He kissed them both. "No. It's the best *family* ever."

* * * * *

Next month THE BRIDES OF BELLA ROSA
*continues as Scarlett Gibson returns to Monta
Correnti to take charge of the Rosa restaurant…
and ends up coming face to face with a
blast from her past, chef Lorenzo Nesta.
Sparks will be flying in the kitchen!*

Look out for
PASSIONATE CHEF, ICE QUEEN BOSS
by Jennie Adams

HARLEQUIN® *Romance*.

Coming Next Month

Available September 14, 2010

#4189 AUSTRALIA'S MOST ELIGIBLE BACHELOR
Margaret Way
The Rylance Dynasty

#4190 PASSIONATE CHEF, ICE QUEEN BOSS
Jennie Adams
The Brides of Bella Rosa

#4191 ACCIDENTALLY PREGNANT!
Rebecca Winters
Mediterranean Dads

#4192 SPARKS FLY WITH MR. MAYOR
Teresa Carpenter

#4193 WEDDING DATE WITH THE BEST MAN
Melissa McClone
Girls' Weekend in Vegas

#4194 DESERTED ISLAND, DREAMY EX!
Nicola Marsh
The Fun Factor

REQUEST YOUR FREE BOOKS!
2 FREE NOVELS PLUS 2
FREE GIFTS!

HARLEQUIN® *Romance*.

From the Heart, For the Heart

YES! Please send me 2 FREE Harlequin® Romance novels and my 2 FREE gifts (gifts are worth about $10). After receiving them, if I don't wish to receive any more books, I can return the shipping statement marked "cancel". If I don't cancel, I will receive 6 brand-new novels every month and be billed just $3.32 per book in the U.S. or $3.72 per book in Canada. That's a savings of at least 26% off the cover price! It's quite a bargain! Shipping and handling is just 50¢ per book.* I understand that accepting the 2 free books and gifts places me under no obligation to buy anything. I can always return a shipment and cancel at any time. Even if I never buy another book, the two free books and gifts are mine to keep forever.

116/316 HDN E5NS

Name _____ (PLEASE PRINT) _____

Address _____ Apt. # _____

City _____ State/Prov. _____ Zip/Postal Code _____

Signature (if under 18, a parent or guardian must sign)

Mail to the **Harlequin Reader Service:**
IN U.S.A.: P.O. Box 1867, Buffalo, NY 14240-1867
IN CANADA: P.O. Box 609, Fort Erie, Ontario L2A 5X3

Not valid for current subscribers to Harlequin Romance books.

**Are you a subscriber to Harlequin Romance books
and want to receive the larger-print edition?
Call 1-800-873-8635 today!**

HR10R

HARLEQUIN®

A Romance

FOR EVERY MOOD™

Spotlight on
Heart & Home

Heartwarming romances
where love can happen
right when you least expect it.

See the next page to enjoy a sneak peek
from Harlequin Superromance®,
a Heart and Home series.

CATHHHSRI0

Enjoy a sneak peek at fan favorite Molly O'Keefe's
Harlequin Superromance miniseries,
THE NOTORIOUS O'NEILLS, *with*
TYLER O'NEILL'S REDEMPTION,
available September 2010
only from Harlequin Superromance.

Police chief Juliette Tremblant recognized the shape of the man strolling down the street—in as calm and leisurely fashion as if it were the middle of the day rather than midnight. She slowed her car, convinced her eyes were playing tricks on her. It had been a long time since Tyler O'Neill had been seen in this town.

As she pulled to a stop at the curb, he turned toward her, and her heart about stopped.

"What the hell are you doing here, Tyler?"

"Well, if it isn't Juliette Tremblant." He made his way over to her, then leaned down so he could look her in the eye. He was close enough to touch.

Juliette was not, repeat, *not* going to touch Tyler O'Neill. Not with her fingers. Not with a ten-foot pole. There would be no touching. Which was too bad, since it was the only way she was ever going to convince herself the man standing in front of her—as rumpled and heart-stoppingly handsome now as he'd been at sixteen—was real.

And not a figment of all her furious revenge dreams.

"What are you doing back in Bonne Terre?" she asked.

"The manor is sitting empty," Tyler said and shrugged, as though his arriving out of the blue after ten years was casual. "Seems like someone should be watching over the family home."

"You?" She laughed at the very notion of him being here for any unselfish reason. "Please."

He stared at her for a second, then smiled. Her heart fluttered against her chest—a small mechanical bird powered by that smile.

"You're right." But that cryptic comment was all he offered.

Juliette bit her lip against the other questions.

Why did you go?

Why didn't you write? Call?

What did I do?

But what would be the point? Ten years of silence were all the answer she really needed.

She had sworn off feeling anything for this man long ago. Yet one look at him and all the old hurt and rage resurfaced as though they'd been waiting for the chance. That made her mad.

She put the car in gear, determined not to waste another minute thinking about Tyler O'Neill. "Have a good night, Tyler," she said, liking all the cool "go screw yourself" she managed to fit into those words.

It seems Juliette has an old score to settle with Tyler.
Pick up TYLER O'NEILL'S REDEMPTION
to see how he makes it up to her.
Available September 2010,
only from Harlequin Superromance.

Love Inspired

Fan Favorite

Janet Tronstad

brings readers a heartwarming story
of love and hope with

Dr. Right

Treasure Creek, Alaska, has only one pediatrician:
the very handsome, very eligible Dr. Alex Haven.
With his contract coming to an end, he plans
to return home to Los Angeles. But Nurse
Maryann Jenner is determined to keep Alex
in Alaska, and when a little boy's life—and
Maryann's hope—is jeopardized, Alex may
find a reason to stay forever.

ALASKAN *Bride* RUSH

Available September wherever books are sold.

Steeple
Hill®

www.SteepleHill.com

LI87620

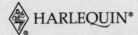

MARGARET WAY

introduces

THE *Rylance* DYNASTY

The lives & loves of Australia's most powerful family

Growing up in the spotlight hasn't been easy, but the two Rylance heirs, Corin and his sister, Zara, have come of age and are ready to claim their inheritance. Though they are privileged, proud and powerful, they are about to discover that there are some things money can't buy....

Look for:

Australia's Most Eligible Bachelor
Available September

Cattle Baron Needs a Bride
Available October